Finding Opa!

The Lonely Heart Series

Latrivia S. Nelson

RH
RIVERHOUSE
PUBLISHING

Finding Opa!

RiverHouse Publishing, LLC
5100 Poplar Avenue
Suite 2700
Memphis, TN 38117

All **RiverHouse, LLC** Titles, Imprints and Distributed Lines are available at special quantity discounts for bulk purchases for sales promotions, premiums, fund-raising and educational or institutional use.

First RiverHouse, LLC Trade Paperback Printing: 08/01/2011

1

ISBN: 978-0-9832186-9-2
ISBN: 0-9832-1869-2

Printed in the United States of America

This book is printed on acid-free paper.

www.riverhousepublishingllc.com

This book is dedicated to every woman who has guarded her heart because of tragedy. May you one day find your Opa.

What does the Greek word "Opa" mean? *According to some it is a word or pronouncement of celebration; the celebration of life itself. It is another way of expressing joy and gratitude to God, life, and others, for bringing one into the state of ultimate wisdom.*

Dear Reader,

This is the second book from The Lonely Heart Series. I'm sure that you'll see that Stacey and Hunter's story is unique and much different from anything I've written before. This story focuses on recovering from loss and learning to love again.

There are so many people who find the *perfect love*, a person that they plan to spend the rest of their lives with, but a freak accident or a horrible thing happens, and they are left alone again. It's a horrific thing that leaves you feeling like a part of you died with them. Then, replacing that lover is one of the hardest and bravest things a person can do to recover. But these characters do it, despite the many obstacles.

Now, you know I like to write about scenarios that are not necessarily the "norm." Call me crazy, but it is fun to think outside of the box. You'll probably admonish me a few times in this book, because of how I allow the characters to behave. But the joy of writing a story, in my opinion, is being able to create the flaws that make people human...fallible. How else are we to learn if we never make mistakes?

My mind was in a different place when I wrote this. I thought of rainy weather, a city by the sea, bikes, beer, local pubs, urban settings and a special couple who loves to wake up next to each other in the morning. I wanted them to be successful in every way except for love, because I wanted to prove that money doesn't buy happiness.

I hope you like my story, and while I'm not sure that it will change your life, I'm sure that it will at least entertain you. Sure, you might say that "I would never get caught in that situation," but it is my goal for you to at least see how they did.

Thanks for being a supporter of my work. Enjoy!

Latrivia S. Nelson

Acknowledgments

I'd like to thank my wonderful team at River-House Publishing for your dedication and support, for your countless hours of work and your shared vision of where this company can go in the future.

To my wonderful husband and family, thanks for continuing to be patient, loving and kind.

To Karen Moss, who has been a wonderful God-send by helping me clean up my manuscripts, thank you for seeing something special in me.

Chapter One

Seattle, Washington

Sitting in the back of T.W. Milligan's pub near ten o'clock on a dreary Wednesday night, Stacey worked alone in her booth on her netbook. She had been there for hours in the smoke-filled bar pouring her thoughts into her computer and trying to develop the perfect story. But so far nothing meaningful had hit her because of a dreadful writer's block. As she ordered another beer, she finally took her fingers off the black keys and yawned.

Manclasting Publishing wanted a *romance novel* that would knock readers' socks off, and all she could come up with were pages of scenery and boring soliloquy. It was dramatically pathetic and a far cry from her first novel.

When she released her debut novel, *Love Knocks*, she hadn't expected such a warm welcome into the industry, but within two months of her drop date, she had soared onto the *Essence Book Club* top ten books as well as the *USA Today* best-sellers list.

Since then, she had not released a single book, had not written a single word. Sure, she had tried, but the keyboard was like a foreign object to her. Her thoughts were not her own anymore.

However, Stacey was under contract with Manclasting and two months from her most important deadline yet. Whatever writing block was standing in her way now, she had to get past it. More than money was on the line, her entire reputation hung in the balance.

Interrupting Stacey's thoughts on her current dilemma, a young, familiar brunette waitress brought over Stacey's cheese dip, placed it on the wooden table in front of her and picked up her empty bottles.

"Got anything, yet?" the waitress asked with a smile.

"Nothing," Stacey replied, picking up her fresh bottle of Red Stripe. The perspiration on the bottle wet her fingers as she stroked the neck. "I normally write a good story when I'm half-cocked," she joked. "But I just don't have the passion, you know." She shrugged, hating the idea of becoming a one-hit wonder.

"I'm sure something will come to ya," the waitress said as she nodded and walked away.

Stacey knew that she could hope, but the truth of the matter was that it was nearly impossible for her to write about world-wind romances when she was as lonely as a woman could be.

The only thing that could be remotely considered a *companion* in her life was her Abyssinian cat, Rapture. And the only thing that could be considered remotely exciting in her life was her weekly Zumba class, which had recently ended.

Outside of that, Stacey Lane Bryant was ridiculously boring.

"Let's get back to it," she ordered herself aloud as she placed her bottle beside her and cracked her knuckles.

She touched the laptop again, savoring the way the keys felt under her fingers. *Love is a covetous word*, she wrote, *a word that encompasses man's reason for living, for dying and for all the hopes in his life*." Even as she wrote the words, she felt the hole inside of her swelling. How was she to write about this when love was the one thing that she was missing?

Frustrated, she stopped again. "This is going nowhere," she growled. It wasn't the words that she didn't believe; it was the words that hurt her to her core. It had been two years since *the car crash*, and yet she still could only think of Drew.

He was ever-present on her mind, still alive in her thoughts and in everything that she did. Every joy and every pain that she had experienced since him was always coupled with the thought of how different it would be if he was still alive.

Drew Hampton had been Stacey's everything. They were married, in love and inseparable – so inseparable in fact that he had insisted on going with her to a book signing across town because of the pouring rain. She remembered that night like it was yesterday.

When the truck that hit them collided with their car, it mangled the passenger side. And while she was knocked unconscious, she only sustained minor injuries. Drew, however, died instantly.

If he had not ridden with her, he would still be alive. That was a fact that she grappled with daily. They would still be married, probably have kids, and definitely be happy. Now, she was alone at 32 years old without a husband, without a family and definitely without happiness. It just did not seem fair.

Tears started to form, burning as it mingled with her mascara. Batting profusely, she grabbed a napkin and dapped her lower lids. *Not the crying again*, she quietly admonished. People would think that she was drunk. She would make a spectacle of herself.

"Can I buy you a drink?" a deep baritone voice asked. "Something to cheer you up?"

"No, I think I'm drunk enough," Stacey answered sarcastically as she looked up. Butterflies erupted immediately in the pit of her stomach. The man was an Adonis, which was rare for this pub.

Staring back down at her while leaning on the booth's wooden side, a man in a gray cotton t-shirt smiled at Stacey, revealing perfect white teeth under full lips made for kissing. "You sure?" he asked, sitting down across from her without permission. "You look like you could use a drink or someone to talk to."

Stacey watched him carefully. He reeked of confidence and expensive cologne. "I'm sure," she said shortly. "But I'll buy you a drink to get up from my table." She didn't know why she had just said that. She didn't mean it. In fact, it was probably *just* what she needed.

The man sat quietly for a moment with a cunning grin on his face, reading through her false wall. His unnaturally green eyes had a devilish sparkle in them, as if he knew something that she didn't. "Okay, I'd like a seven and seven *to go*," he said, resting his large muscular arm back on the edge of the seat. Veins shot through his sinewy, tanned form from the joints of his arms to his wrists.

Work out much? Stacey thought to herself as she sat quietly.

The waitress walked back up with a grin on her face, and suddenly Stacey knew that she was being set up.

Everyone at T.W. Milligans knew Stacey and her macabre story. They all knew that she didn't accept drinks or buy drinks for anyone. She didn't pick up men or give out her phone number. The pub was her place of relaxation. She could catch the game, be around people, and have a few drinks then walk or ride home – alone.

"You want a drink, darling?" the waitress asked the stranger.

It was obvious to Stacey that she wasn't the only one attracted to the guy. Heads around the pub had turned toward them like he was releasing a primal pheromone. He had his own personal scent of sexy.

Okay, Stacey thought to herself, *he's attracting way too much attention.*

His deep baritone tickled at Stacey's senses. "The lady has decided to buy me a seven and seven to get me out of her presence," the stranger said, revealing deep dimples as he smiled.

"Seven and seven coming up," the waitress said, turning to Stacey. "What about you?" Her pen hit the pad in the palm of her hand as she waited.

"I'll have the same," Stacey answered, rolling her eyes. This guy thought that he was clever.

As the waitress walked away, Stacey turned back to the mysterious man. "When your drink arrives, pick it up and leave, please."

"Okay," he said, extending his hand across the table. "In the meantime, I'm Hunter, and you are?" His eyebrow rose like he was *James Bond*, a sign of definite machismo.

Stacey hesitated before she took his hand. "Stacey," she answered, feeling his large, warm hand swallow hers. She pulled away and put her laptop in her backpack, and completely gave up on any hopes of writing. "The way you collect free drinks is very smooth," she said on an exhalation as though she had him all figured out.

"Thank you," he said, watching her as she fidgeted with her things. "I picked the skill up in college."

"Ahh. The way that you let people know that you have some education is clever also," she said, wiping her eyes again with the napkin. More black mascara rubbed off on the paper.

"Women these days don't like their men stupid," he answered, noting her solemn state. "So, what are you writing on your little computer?"

"A love story," she answered, waiting on him to ask a million questions as many men did when they tried to pick her up in the same fashion.

"A love story? That's cool." Hunter looked around the bar and sat back in the booth, getting more comfortable. "Are you an author or something?"

"Yep," Stacey answered coolly. "Look, I'm really not in the mood to be...*picked up*. I bought your drink. Okay. Now, you can leave me alone."

Why was she pushing him away? He was gorgeous. She always did this - always went for the jugular before giving a man a chance. And this one in particular was strangely more attractive than any before him. Shaking her head at her thoughts, she sighed and resisted the natural urge to flare up.

"I'm sorry. You don't deserve that. It's just that I'm so frustrated. I'm on a deadline, and I'm behind schedule. So, I would really appreciate the privacy," she explained exasperated. Her eyes pleaded with him as she frowned, hoping he would just take the hint and leave.

The waitress put down their drinks, giving him his cue to depart, but Hunter didn't budge. Something in the form of admiration flickered in his eyes. "Maybe I can help you in some way. What's your problem?" he asked.

His tone was sincere, which calmed the beast in Stacey for a minute. Letting down her guard, she decided to just tell the guy. What did she have to lose?

"Okay," she said, sitting back in her seat and putting her hands in her lap. "I have writer's block. You see, I need to write a passionate love story, but I can't. And I think it's because I don't have any passion anymore, *at least not for love*. So, I'm stuck, and I only have two months to write this epic manuscript that would rival the Greek love stories spawn by Aphrodite herself, only I have no muse and absolutely no motivation." She blinked hard. Hearing herself finally vocalize her problems only made the invisible weight heavier on her shoulders.

Hunter laughed. It was odd to him that she would refer to the Greeks when speaking of love.

Stacey automatically misinterpreted his laugh. She had just poured out her heart to him, and he didn't take her the least bit serious. Irritated, she growled. "So, how in the hell could you possibly help me, unless you have a loose manuscript in those incredibly tight jeans of yours?"

"Well, that depends," he said, looking down at his pants. He didn't think his jeans were tight, but at least her statement meant that she was checking him out. His large elbows were planted on the table, giving a better view of his sculpted forearms and the chrome Cartier watch on his wrist, gleaming under the light. "When you say that you don't have a muse, does that mean that you're single?" His tone was suggestive. The inflection in his voice was just a tad bit playful.

"My husband died," Stacey answered flatly, countering his flirtatious demeanor. "He's gone." She nodded as sympathy washed Hunter's beautiful face. "So, I have no reason to write elegant stories about whimsical love anymore, because I don't' have a love anymore. I'm not single. I'm widowed. There is a difference, at least in my mind."

"How long?" he asked more serious than before.

"Two *miserable* years, three months and five days."

"And you haven't dated since he passed?" His question was filled with sincerity, like he actually cared about her feelings.

"I haven't tried." She felt the need again to fight back tears.

"I see." Hunter sat back. "Well, there's your problem and your answer. You need a love interest – a *muse* as you so eloquently put it - to help ignite your passion again so that you can finish this book. Then when it's over, you can get rid of him. Think of it as a creative booster."

Stacey laughed aloud. The thought was preposterous. "How many have *you* had to drink tonight?" she asked, taking a sip of her drink. *This guy was more ridiculous than her non-romantic love story.*

"Just a couple." He smiled. Leaning towards her, he made his plea. "I think that I should be your muse. I'm willing to give myself over to the science of love in the effort to help you with your book."

His suggestion floored her. Deflated, she slouched her thin shoulders and squinted her tired eyes. "Are you serious?" she asked. "You don't know anything about me. For all you know, I could be a nut or vice versa."

"Oh, come on. People do it every day. They see each other. They are attracted to one another. They begin to date, and often enough they break up. But they serve a purpose, stay a season. What do you have to lose?" he asked.

"You said that they have to be attracted to one another, right? What makes you think that I would be attracted to you?" she asked intrigued. Her heart skipped a beat as she watched the twinkle in his eye. She did find him attractive – any woman would.

He lowered his sultry voice. "Well, you did let me sit down."

"I was only being nice." Involuntarily, she felt herself flirting.

"I see. Well, there is only one way to solve this. Do you find me attractive, Stacey?" The muscles along his jaw line tightened.

She couldn't help but smile. "Yes," she answered, running her finger over the rim of her glass. "For a white boy."

"Oh..." he laughed. "I need more melanin; is that it?"

She laughed also, forgetting about her book and Drew for a brief moment. "Hey, that could be one strike against you for all you know. The second strike would be making me buy your drink."

"Just as long as I don't strike out, I'm okay. Because I see a beautiful Nubian princess in front of me, and I would hate to miss out," he answered.

"Oh, then on top of that you purposefully played the race card," she said, shaking her head. His humor was so refreshing until she almost considered it. Almost.

"What's your number? Maybe I could give you a call..." he started to say before she cut him off.

"I don't give out my number." Eyeing his napkin, she shut down.

"Well, how am I going to get in touch with you?" he asked, picking up the pen sitting on the edge of the table.

The reality of what he was suggesting set in for Stacey, and she instantly pulled back. "This isn't going to happen," she said, looking down at her hands.

Suddenly, the sounds of the bar were back, drowning her thoughts and dragging her back into her reality. *What am I doing*, she asked herself.

Hunter picked up on the disconnect and made one last-ditch effort to close the deal. "Well, let me give you my number."

Stacey had heard enough. She didn't like the way this guy made her feel with his warm eyes, wide mouth, strong jaw and devilish charm. Maybe it was that she had been drinking far too long, but maybe, just maybe this guy had sparked something deep inside of her. Either way, it was alarming.

"*Oooookay*," she said, looking down at her watch. "Look at the time. I've gotta go."

"But you haven't even considered my proposal," he countered eagerly.

"What are you – a salesman?" she asked, pulling herself up from her seat. "This was fun. But I'm not interested. Trust me; your little pitch is pretty cute. I'm sure that it will work on someone, just not me." She threw down the money on the table.

"What would work on you, I wonder," he said finally.

"The world will never know." Throwing her backpack over her shoulder, she looked over at him once more and raised her brow. "It was *strange* to meet you, Hunter" she said, pulling her sandy brown dreadlocks behind her ear.

Hunter swallowed hard, still gazing at her with his dreamy green eyes. "It was *awesome* to meet you, Stacey. I assure you that I've never made a pitch like that to anyone woman. You are the first," he said, raising his drink to salute her. "And thanks for the free booze. I'll make sure to pick up your novel the next time I'm in the book store."

"Gee, thanks," she said sarcastically.

Waving at the waitress and bartender, who sat across the room at the bar watching, Stacey walked away from the table.

She was certain that the stranger was still watching her, still trying to figure out an angle. But she didn't turn back. Instead, she kept her eyes on the door. Who was she kidding anyway? Anything that sounded too good to be true often was. Her father had one saying he had used repeatedly when she was a child that came to mind now: *Caveat emptor for sure, baby.*

***

The cool rainwater soaked Stacey as she gripped the sides of her green North Face backpack and hiked several blocks up the waterfront to her lonely loft.

With each step she took in the briny air, feeling it jet into her lungs and feed her body, her buzz began to wear off, but the thoughts of Hunter did not. She wondered if she had just made a huge mistake by turning him down or if she had saved herself from a ridiculous situation.

That was the strange thing about life. Sometimes, there was no clear answer. Right now, Hunter could be back at the bar using the same line on another woman, or he could have been seriously interested in only her and went home alone. One thing was for sure. She would never know.

As she hit the steps of her dark bricked building, she looked up to her front window two stories above to see her cat looking down at her. It never failed, and never ceased to amaze Stacey. She swore that Rapture could sense her a hundred miles away. *Who said that dogs were more faithful?*

Wiping the rainwater from her face, she stomped her brown hiking boots on the black, plastic welcome mat at the base of the lobby door and slipped her key in the lock. With a twist of her wrist, she was safely inside out of the elements and standing face-to-face with Clive Blackstone.

Stacey wasn't sure if Blackstone was Clive's real surname, but it definitely fit him. Stuck in the grudge-age and devoted to heavy metal, the part-time guitarist and full-time IT tech, was hopelessly pulled between two worlds.

If Stacey saw Clive from 8-5, Monday through Friday, he was in belted jeans, a button down and clean hair. However, after hours, he wore black eyeliner, a tattered, Matrix-like trench coat and gel-slicked hair that only further pronounced his receding hairline. She found his duality strange but refreshing. At least he had the balls to fly his freak colors.

"Hello, Clive," she said, moving out of the doorway to let him pass with his arms full of equipment. "It's raining out there. You may want to pull your car around first," she suggested.

"It's cool," he said drably, already in character for tonight's performance. "Thanks though."

Stacey always wondered if he got into character to perform at the clubs or if he got into character to perform at work. Closing the door behind him, she decided not to give another moment of thought to Clive or his complex existence.

After a short trip up her elevator to the second floor, she exited out to her front door and stomped her feet again on her own welcome mat before she dashed inside. As she opened her doors, Rapture was right there to gracefully swirl in between her legs with his arched back offered to freely rub.

"Missed you too, cat," she said, closing the door behind her. Dropping her backpack in the corner, she kneeled and picked up her friend, rubbing its fur against her face as she walked over to the table in her living room to listen to her missed messages.

Pushing down on the blinking red button, she heard the message that she had been dreading for days.

"Well, hello, hello," the female, east coast caller said over the machine. "I expected to find you home working on that wonderful manuscript you promised me," her agent, Valerie Morrow, said in a demanding tone. "Call me when you get home. I don't care what time. I just need to know that you're *on schedule.*"

Stacey looked at her cat and shook her head. "I've got to pull something out of my ass quickly, or I'm going to need to move into the litter box with you, Rapture," she said, kissing her cat on the nose. A quick, warm lick from the cat was returned for her favor.

Stacey picked up her cordless phone and walked with her cat in her arms to the kitchen to make a cup of ginger tea. Her agent picked up on the first ring.

"How's my favorite author?" Valerie asked with too much energy for so late at night.

"Not so well," Stacey answered, putting her pewter-colored kettle on the stove. "I have writer's block."

There was a brief silence on the phone. "Well, what do you need to get you motivated? A trip? A new car?"

"A new man," Stacey laughed. "I'll figure it out," she said, thinking involuntarily of Hunter. "Let me send you what I have tomorrow afternoon. I have an appointment in the morning with my new OBGYN."

"It's a date," Valerie said, getting what she needed. "Well, I'll talk to you then, doll. Call me if you need anything."

"I will," Stacey said, hanging up the phone.

Rapture ran his furry head against Stacey's neck as she put the phone down. Smiling, Stacey purred like a cat. "I love you, too."

Chapter Two

Commuting in Seattle could be very difficult if one didn't use public transportation, drive a car or use cabs. In this case, the one in question was Stacey. So she tried to make sure that everything that she needed was in a twenty-mile radius of her home to ensure that she could either ride her bike or drive her plum-colored Vespa.

However, considering that it rained a lot, she often arrived to all of her engagements soaking wet and somewhat irritable. It was days like this one, sunny and clear, that she wished would last forever. If she could find a place that was perpetually tranquil, she'd move there forever.

Dr. H. C. Fourakis had come highly recommended on several accredited websites. Due for an annual checkup, she wondered why she even bothered to go considering she had not been sexually active since the Stone Age. The only thing that was pushing her was the knowledge of how real cervical cancer could be and her desire to be cleared of all possibilities. Her mother had died when she was very young of cervical cancer, and since then she had religiously gone to the doctor for checkups.

Pulling up to the small, bricked building on the corner lot of the busy intersection, she looked up gratefully at the skies that were blue and bright. At least the day had started off right. Maybe, *just maybe*, she could find a reason to write today. She knew that it was hardly possible; yet she clung to the prospect.

Taking her backpack inside with her, she walked up to the reception desk, checked in and had a seat in the half-full waiting room. It was a nice little practice, clean and modern with lots of abstract art and health pamphlets strategically placed around the well-lit space.

Grabbing the current issue of *Vogue* magazine on the table across from her, she flipped through the pages blankly until she heard her named call.

"That was fast," Stacey said, standing up. Waving at the nurse, she quickly made her way back to a small, sterile white room and put her backpack on the floor in the corner.

The nurse was quick with her chores of checking her blood pressure, going through the questionnaire and taking her blood. When she was done, she informed Stacey that the doctor would be in to see her momentarily; so she would need to change out of her clothes and into the blue, paper examination gown on the table.

Taking her time after she was left alone, Stacey pulled off her favorite, distressed jeans and t-shirt, boots and socks, and made a neatly folded pile in the chair.

Sitting on the small bed, she looked around the room with her hands clasped as she listened to the people move about outside the door. She always got nervous at the doctor's office, and the result was often itchy, sweaty underarms. Running her thumb under her wet arm pit, she took a deep breath and rested back on the examination table.

Knock. Knock. She sat up as the door opened. *Showtime.* The mysterious Dr. H. C. Fourakis walked in with a clipboard in-hand and closed the door behind him.

"Good afternoon, Ms. Bryant," he greeted, looking up from his paperwork.

"I don't believe it," Stacey said flabbergasted. "*You* are Dr. H. C. Fourakis? As in *Hunter, the drink hustler?*" She didn't know whether to laugh or cry. Life could be so cruelly ironic at times. He would die if he knew that she actually went to bed thinking about him the night before.

Hunter put down his blue clipboard and tried to wipe the devious grin from his face. "In the flesh," he said, leaning against the workstation across from her. "This is how I pay the bills. The drink hustling is my night gig." His brows pinched down as he studied her.

"You're an OB/GYN?" She shook her head in disbelief. Go figure.

"It's a family practice actually. My dad was the first. My sister and I run it now. So, you see there is really no need for me to be too boisterous. I'm just playing copycat here." He sat down on the white stool in the corner and pulled a sleek silver pen from his white smock. "So, what are we doing today?"

Stacey pulled her little paper gown around her, uncomfortable with being nude with a man who had tried to pick her up twelve hours before. "*We* are not doing anything. If your sister isn't available, then I'll change doctors with my insurance company and reschedule for a later date somewhere else with someone else. But there is no way in hell that I'm going to let you..." She didn't bother to finish her statement, certain that he understood her concern.

Both of their eyes wondered to her covered vagina.

"Well, I don't want to lose your business. I'll see if Hanna is available," he said, standing up. He walked over to the door and stopped. With a quick turn in his brown loafers, he faced her. "I hope you won't let last night effect your impression of our practice. We're very professional here and devoted to women's healthcare."

Stacey slumped down on the bed and shook her head. "I'll give your sister a chance," she said, feeling sorry for him. "Just hurry up before I change my mind."

Hunter put up his hands and smiled. "Great," he said, showing his dimples. "She'll be right in, and I'm leaving right now."

***

An hour later, after Dr. Hanna Fourakis, an equally attractive and young likeness of her brother, had seen her, Stacey emerged from the doctor's office with a positive experience minus the encounter with Hunter, *the drink hustling OB/GYN.*

Slipping on her backpack, she mounted her Vespa and prepared to head home when a black Toyota 4runner pulled in front of her.

"Hey, did everything turn out cool?" Hunter asked, taking off his shades.

"*Turn out cool?*" Stacey smirked. "Are doctors supposed to talk like that?"

"Like what?" Hunter asked. Putting the car in park, he opened the door and stepped out in a pair of jeans and a gray polo.

His copper-colored, curly hair and deep-tanned skin made Stacey curious. He looked like a model. There was no way that he wasn't a Casanova. "What kind of name is *Fourakis*?" she asked, slipping on her plum-colored helmet.

"Greek," he said proudly, although she said it like a curse word. "What kind of name is Bryant?"

"Slave owner name, I suppose," she said with an obnoxious growl. "Well, have a great day." Her tone was less than harmonious.

"Wait," Hunter said, putting his hand on her bike. He tilted his head and smiled. "Let me take you for lunch. It's the least that I could do, considering that I've been such a pest."

"I have to write a book or did you forget? And yes, you have been a total pest." She kept her eyes on his hand.

"Why are you playing so hard to get? I just want to take you out, get to know you better. Is that so much to ask?" he pleaded. His grip was tighter on her handle bars.

"Look Hunter," she said huffing. Flicking his fingers off her handles, she stood straddling her bike. "I'm not a young girl with plenty of time to waste. I don't like games. Do I find you attractive? Like I told you last night, yes, I do. But I don't have time for this...not now. I'm *busy*," she hissed.

He moved closer to her, determined to change her mind. "I'm not playing games. I'm trying to take you to lunch." He looked into her eyes and bit his lip again. His attraction to her was obvious. "I like you. I don't know why. I saw you at the bar last night on your little computer, and you just seemed different, like a breath of fresh air. So, I figured that since you are single, and I'm single what would be the harm. You know me better now. You know where I work. You know what I do. We're even. Right?"

Stacey smiled despite herself. Looking across the street at the seafood deli, she shook her head. "Yeah. Okay."

He raised his brow. Did this little *hard ass* actually agree with something that he said? "Is that a yes?" he asked for more clarification.

"*Yeah, okay.* We can go across the street to lunch right now." She pointed across the way. "Over there." The smell of food wafted across the street to them. The place looked safe and harmless enough, and she had a taste for fish and chips. Essentially, she could kill two birds with one stone.

"Great. Hop in and I'll drive you across." His keys jingled in his hand.

"Oh, I don't do cars," she said, pushing her Vespa. "Go on. I'll meet you across there."

"You don't do *cars*?" he asked confused. "Do you drive that thing everywhere?"

"Do you or do you not want this date, drink hustler?" she asked, refusing to explain.

"Alright. Alright. I'll see you across there," he said, getting back into his truck.

***

Sitting across from each other in a booth next to the window facing towards the breathtaking waterfront, Stacey and Hunter finally had a chance to talk. Fresh crab cakes, hot fish and chips, spaghetti, coleslaw and iced tea lined the small wooden table for two and gave her ample space to prevent the date from feeling too intimate.

As the waitress brought out extra condiments, Stacey sat back in her seat and pursed her lips together. "This doesn't add up. Out of the blue last night, you walked up to my booth and tried to pick me up. And today could have very well been coincidental, *if there is such a thing*, but something tells me that it wasn't. You care to explain?"

He laughed nervously, indicating that her suspicions were correct. Clearing his throat, he tried to give his side of the story. "Yesterday was the anniversary of my wife's long journey to death. And it's always very difficult for me. So, I try to go places that we used to hang out together in order to remember what my life used to be like."

Stacey frowned. She wasn't expecting something so morbid. Disarmed, she relaxed her protective body language and waited to understand what his wife's death had to do with her.

Hunter looked down at his vacant ring finger. "First, let me catch you up to speed. My wife couldn't pay for medical school outright like my parents did for me, so she joined the Army and ended up in Iraq shortly after graduation from medical school. The theatre hospital where she was working was hit under attack by insurgents, and she was transferred to Walter Reed in DC for treatment where she fought for her life for two months and six days before she passed away."

Stacey didn't blink but her face had definitely warmed with compassion. She loved the military as much as the next citizen and sympathized with anyone who had been killed trying to serve the country.

Hunter tried to smile, but the pain was evident on his face. "I never left her side when she was returned to the states. Day in and day out, I watched her tortured in pain, fighting to survive. She said that she didn't want to leave me without a family of our own. So, the idea of healing and having a baby was what gave her hope and kept her alive for so long. Plus, the staff at the burn unit were amazing. But in the end, they couldn't save her. No one could. Infection set in and she finally succumbed."

Tears ran down Stacey's face. For the first time, she realized that someone had been through more than she and Drew, and the reality of that fact was both overwhelming and refreshing. Because at that moment, she knew that she wasn't alone. However, she was also very ashamed of how poorly she had handled her own misfortune.

Hunter continued in a deeper more solemn voice, "Anyway, her favorite pub was T.W. Milligan's, and I go there every year on the day that she was sent to Walter Reed, and I normally don't stop going there until the two months and six days are over. Needless to say, the bartender knows me well. That is why I was there last night."

Stacey sighed, putting two and two together. Greg knew her story too. On many nights after Drew's death, Greg had called her a cab when she had drunk herself into a mindless stupor.

"Good ole' Greg," he said, shaking his head. He ran his finger around his glass rim. "And while I was about to get blasted to try and take some of the hurt away, he told me that I wasn't alone, *not even the bar*, and told me your story." He wiped his face with his right hand and raised it. With a smile, he continued. "So, I turned and I saw you, and I understood the tears in your eyes, and for the first time since my wife passed away, I made a play for a different woman. It wasn't easy though, and I think we can both say that my *mad skills* are lacking."

Stacey's face was unreadable. Looking into his eyes, she finally let out a breath. "I don't know what to say."

"Don't be mad," he pleaded. "Last night, talking to you was the most exciting thing that I've done in a long time. For a minute, looking into your eyes, trying to get on your good side, hoping maybe that you'd bite – I don't know – it made me feel alive again. It made me feel like maybe there was a better way to spend two months and six days of my life."

Stacey looked down at the table, embarrassed that she had been so cold to him before. In the past, she had always prided herself on being humble and just, but last night was a testament to her ability to still be a bitch. She had to fix this – reboot.

"Last night, did you really want to be my muse?" she asked.

"Yes, of course I did...I do," he answered quickly.

He marveled at her. Stacey Bryant was clearly one of kind - tall, slender, dark silky skin, wide-brown eyes that looked like they carried the world in them, lips full and pouty with only a faint hint of gloss, a smile that burned deep in his chest to his soul and long, sandy-brown dreadlocks that hit the middle of her perfect back. She was a goddess. Who wouldn't want to spend time with her?

Hunter tied up all loose ends. "And I had no idea that you'd end up in my office today. I swear that was completely coincidental, *if there is such a thing*," he vowed, though he wasn't much for coincidences either.

Stacey liked the way that he was looking at her now, and she believed him. She could sense that he was hurting as badly as she. Only two people who had lost someone they loved well before their time could understand the absolute and utter emptiness that something like that caused.

"Any kids?" she asked, trying to move past their sad moment.

"No. You?"

"No," she answered with a bit of relief and remorse. At thirty-two, she always thought that she would have kids. It was funny how life deviated from her plans. "Well, let's see how this date goes, and if it ends well, then we can start on our little project tomorrow, if you still want to," she said, nearly in a whisper with her chin tucked in.

"*Sotto voce*," Hunter said, "I'd like very much."

"With a few guidelines of course," she added, before she forgot herself.

"Understandable." He nodded and waited.

"When I say stop, we stop. No questions asked."

"Of course." He saluted her.

"No sex," she bit out.

He paused. "Okay." He smiled, but his hand dropped back down to the table.

"And when the book is done, and your time of mourning is over, then if we want to go our separate ways, there won't be any pressure from either person."

"It'll be our way of helping each other," he added.

"Exactly," she said, taking a sip of tea.

"Exactly," he repeated.

Stacey's gaze landed squarely back on his, and suddenly she wanted to ask if he was wearing contacts. She had never seen irides so green and brilliant. If the eyes were truly doors to the soul, what his soul was like?

***

The bike ride home was absolutely painful for Stacey. Driving as fast as she possibly could on her Vespa, she forgot about the wind in her hair and the beautiful blue skies and jetted to her loft apartment with a mission in mind.

Words, emotions and excitement were swirling through her bloodstream like some potent drug pumped intravenously through her deprived veins. It had been years since she had felt like this, but it was finally back. She wanted to scream aloud, maybe dance a jig. But more than anything, Stacey wanted to write!

Hunter had already invigorated her. She nearly stopped at the park across the street and started to type, but instead, she finished her trek home and dashed inside with Rapture.

Slamming the door and throwing down her helmet, she picked up her cat with both hands. "You'll never believe what happened to me today, kitty," she said in a wispy voice. "I met a man." Her voice strained in disbelief. "A real life man." She held the cat up to her face. "And I think he's the key to writing this freaking novel and getting Val off my back."

Rapture licked her face and purred – the extent of his ability to show enthusiasm.

After turning on her kettle for tea, she opened her curtains to let in the sunshine and plopped down in front of her computer. Grabbing the remote, she turned on her stereo, selected Common's latest CD and began to type. Her nimble fingers could barely keep up with her multiplying thoughts. Deep inside, she was on fire with possibilities and imagination.

Chapter Three

At first dusk, with the windows open and waves of fresh air blowing through his linen curtains, Hunter lay sleeping in his bed naked with only a large white towel wrapped around his carved, tanned waist.

Fidgeting as he dreamt of his wife, sweat beads formed on his forehead and under his lip. Flashes of the woman he loved shook him to his core. Shivering not because of the cool air but because of the quaking trauma of her death, he mumbled her name on his lips then heaved a heavy sigh of defeat.

Even as he slept, *she* haunted him. The memories of his untimely loss overwhelmed him, causing him to ball up his fists in fury. How could a woman so wonderful with so much to give to this world be taken in her prime?

"Why?!!" he cried out as he sat up in the bed. That was a recurring question that had never been answered. *Why did she have to die? Why did she have to leave him? Why couldn't she have survived? Why? Why? Why?*

The rush of adrenaline shot through his veins and quickened the pace of his aching heart. Tears ran down his cheeks in heavy hot drops that salted his lips. Wiping them quickly, he looked around disoriented and realized that he was in the lonely confines of his home. The desolate silence made his reality even more sobering. Batting his watery eyes, he moved out of his nightmare into the present with a bitter resolve.

After seeing his patients, he had darted home to get ready for his date with Stacey. He cleaned his waterfront loft quickly, throwing clothes in baskets and dishes in the dishwater then jumped in the shower.

Honestly, he had fallen asleep feeling rather hopeful. But his thoughts had drifted off towards the woman he had lost, and he had woken up in his normal fashion – alone and frantic.

The bed creaked a little as he pushed his body towards the end of the mattress and sank his feet into the plush rug below. Slumped over, he ran his hands through is hair and tried to calm down. How was he supposed to impress this new woman if he showed up utterly depressed over the old one?

A crisp breeze rushed in and greeted him, reminding him that there was now a lot less time to tarry. Finally finding the strength somewhere in the pit of his soul, he stood up and made his way to his closet, passing the picture of his beloved wife on the nightstand as he went. He stopped and looked at her photo.

"I hope you understand what I'm attempting to do," he said to the photo of her in her wedding gown. "The psychiatrist seems to think that I'm living in the past, but I tried to explain to him that everyone's grieving period is different. I mean, there are men who go decades without dating after their wives pass away."

He could nearly hear her voice respond. "You don't have decades," he could imagine her saying. "What about children? What about a family of your own?"

Hunter knew that it wasn't his wife responding to him but his own silent desires. He wasn't getting any younger. Everyone he knew was at least attempting to build a family. Yet, he was stagnant – dangling in the balance as people passed him by.

More than anything, he wanted to be that dad on the playground with his kid who looked happy because he was happy. He wanted a schedule full of things to do with his own family. Also, he didn't want to be the *attractive but extremely reclusive* bachelor for the rest of his life.

He walked to his closet and pulled out a pair of jeans. "But what if she gets to know me, and she thinks that I'm *absolutely* and *unequivocally* the wrong guy?" Throwing his pants on the bed, he went to his dresser and pulled out a pair of boxers. He threw up his index finger in protest. "Plus, she could only be doing this to write her book, or because she feels sorry for me."

He closed the dresser drawer and looked at himself in the mirror. "I don't know which one would be worse. Either way, I'm going to give this my best shot. So, when it doesn't work, I have an excuse to keep on being alone. And I can tell people that I tried, but I'm just not ready to go back out there again."

Hunter knew that he was setting himself up for failure. To talk down the possibility of a good relationship before he even gave it a chance only proved his own negativity. Plus, there was the nagging fact that he was the one who had pursued her – not the other way around.

Stacey had done him a great service by saying yes, and here he was already prepared for things to go terribly wrong. His conscience ripped at him. *Man up*, it roared.

Even as he tried to convince himself aloud that things wouldn't work, he also couldn't ignore the nervous excitement that made his stomach flutter. There was something about Stacey that seemed off in a good way. She was different and independent, funny and clever. If nothing else, he could at least make a friend. A friend couldn't be bad. He had how many now? Two.

Plus, he just couldn't get her smile out of his mind. When she had agreed to his proposal yesterday at lunch, it was like someone had given him a million dollars. She had looked at him with a sincere hope. Her eyes had said to him that maybe, possibly, he could be the one that would help her move out of her own personal hell. He only hoped that she would also serve as the same stepping stone for him.

For the last two years, he had done nothing but sulk, mourn and pout in solitary. Maybe God had finally answered his prayers by sending him a woman who could understand his pain and possibly knew how to heal him?

He looked at himself in the mirror of his bathroom and stuck out his chest.

Tonight, he was going to pursue Stacey Bryant with everything that he had in him, or he was going to make a complete fool out of himself in front of a bestselling author. *Either way, it was balls to the wall.*

***

Stacey hadn't been on a date in years. Standing in front of her gold-framed mirror, she and her cat analyzed her dress.

"What am I saying in this?" she asked Rapture, turning to view her side profile. Confused, she smoothed her hands over her dress and sighed. "You're supposed to wear a dress on the first date, right?"

The cat looked up at her and meowed.

"I'll take that as a yes," Stacey said, walking into her bathroom. With her toes pointed, she slipped her feet into her pumps and sprayed her perfume.

It had been forever since she had seen herself look like this. Normally, she was in a pair of jeans or cargo pants, coupled with boots, a comfy t-shirt and a backpack full of tech gear. Now, she was wearing Victoria Secret, thigh-highs, stiletto heels and exposing parts of her body that she had not paid attention to in quite some time. It was mildly amusing – two sides to a very sordid coin.

A nervous jitter hit Stacey when she heard the doorbell chime. He was five minutes early! With a quick glance at the wooden clock mounted on the wall, she grabbed her black clutch purse and scampered to the front door, while trying to remember how to walk in heels.

Rapture followed closely behind, feeling the need suddenly to be overly protective of his master. He let out another meow that made her slow down.

She turned to him and sighed. "I know; I'm nervous too, kitty." Avoiding his fur in fear that it might rub off on her black dress, she turned back to the door and opened it.

To her surprise, it was Clive. Slouching over, she looked passed him into the hallway. "What gives, Clive?" She finally eyed him suspiciously.

In his normal black, matrix-like costume, he showed her a CD. "Just came out today. I'm selling them door-to-door. Would you like...no would you mind buying one to support me?"

Stacey took the CD and flipped it around to read the black. "Twisted Fantasies?" she said, looking up at him. "Is it heavy metal?"

"It's alternative rock and roll," he corrected. "You listen to it much?"

Stacey shook her head. "How much?"

"Ten bucks," Clive answered hopeful.

Fishing out her wallet from her purse, she pulled out a ten-dollar bill and gave it to him. "Well, I had better go."

"Got a date?" Clive asked, impressed with his neighbor's sudden transformation. "You look hot."

"Gee, thanks," Stacey said, blushing. "So, I had better go. I may have like five more minutes to put on a little more make-up."

"Okay. Thanks for your support," Clive said, backing away from the door. "And if you only do it once, listen to it. You just might like it. I wrote all of the songs on this one. It's my solo gig. I'm trying to get famous."

As Clive was explaining, the doors to the elevator opened, and Hunter emerged with a huge bouquet of red roses. He stopped in his tracks with a what-the-hell look on his face as he saw Clive with his date.

Stacey waved him over with a smile. "Oh, there he is," Stacey said, feeling her chest tighten at the very sight of him. He looked even better than the first couple of times. Dressed in black, sleek and sexy, he approached with a wicked grin.

Hunter walked past Clive and turned with a curious smile. "How you doing?" Hunter asked, nodding at the oddly dressed man.

"Treat her nice," Clive ordered sternly as he turned awkwardly and headed to the next door with his bag of CDs.

Hunter didn't reply. Instead, he strode over to the door where Stacey stood and looked her up and down. "Wow," he said, lost for words. In his mind, he had never imagined that she would have worn a dress just for him. She was totally a jeans and t-shirt type of girl. And while he didn't mind her normal style, he was incredibly thankful for a glimpse at the most perfect body that he'd ever seen.

"I take it that you like the duds?" Stacey said, rubbing her hand over her dress playfully.

"What straight man wouldn't?" he answered, finally offering the flowers. "These are for you, though they are dramatically diminished by your beauty."

Stacey was caught off guard by his gracious compliment. She took them and smelled their aroma. "They're beautiful," she said, stepping to the side. "Won't you come in?" She fluttered her eyelashes lightheartedly. "I'm playing the debutante thing up tonight."

"Absolutely," he said, walking past her.

Stacey's home was as eclectic as she was, which was a relief to Hunter. He believed that the home should match the soul. Usually, where there was conflict in the two, there was often a person in the middle of an identity crisis. Hers was a sprawling, open loft with exposed brick walls, hanging designer lights, rich colors and culturally meaningful art. He stopped at a painting of Miles Davis and smiled.

"I definitely like the Miles," he said, noting that the piece was an original.

Putting the flowers into a crystal vase, Stacey looked up a nodded. "My father was a saxophonist in Harlem. I grew up listening to Miles Davis and Coltrane. It's in my blood."

Hunter noticed the photos on the wall facing the street. Each was in a black frame, each a black and white photo of Harlem. Some were from the present, others from various decades. All were of musicians at various clubs or congregating together on various corners. He marveled at the paintings, feeling as though they all told a secret story about Stacey that he would never had known if he hadn't bothered to look.

"So you grew up in Harlem?" he asked, turning to steal another glance of her.

Stacey walked to over him. "Yes. New York was my home for many years," she said nostalgically. She looked up at the photos and smiled.

"Do you ever miss it?" Secretly, he inhaled a whiff of her cologne, while keeping his eyes on the wall. It was hard to do with her standing beside him. He wanted to turn and hold her in his arms.

"Sometimes," she answered.

"So, why won't you go back?"

She bit her lip. What was this, twenty questions? "I don't travel," she said, frowning. "I haven't traveled since Drew died."

Normally, her divulging that information would have made another person uncomfortable, but Hunter seemed to understand. He looked at his watch. "Well, should we get on with our date?"

"Sure."

"Great. I *Googled* the area and found a great little Greek restaurant not far from here. It's walking distance."

"I've eaten at nearly every restaurant within a ten-mile radius," she said, walking towards the door. "Is it *Mediterranean Nights*?"

He closed the door behind them. "Yes, do you like it?"

Stacey locked the door and looked up at him. "I love Mediterranean food. I know the owners there too - Mr. and Mrs. Santorini."

"Okay. We'll, *I don't know them*, but if you say it's nice, I'm sure that it is. Plus, that is an awesome last name. Santorini, Greece is home to one of the deadliest volcano eruptions in history."

"Outside of being a drink hustler and a doctor, are you also a historian?" she asked amused.

Hunter laughed. "No, but I love Greek history, Greek culture, Greek everything." His face lit up.

"But not Greek girls?" Stacey asked curiously. Her eyes narrowed at him.

"Oh, I never said that. It's just that I'm not exclusive to any particular type of woman. I just want a good one."

"I like that," Stacey said, adding one more note about him to her mental rolodex. "Proud of who you are but not ethnocentric."

Hunter chuckled.

"Are you sure that you don't mind walking?" Stacey asked reluctantly. Her eyes told on her. She wanted him to be happy. "I would normally ride my bike, but I'm sure that with this dress on it would only be more uncomfortable."

"I don't mind walking at all. I missed hitting the gym today. I could use a little cardio."

"So you're a *glass half full* kind of guy, huh?" she asked curiously. Their feet echoed as they walked through the lobby.

Hunter opened the door for her and watched her move pass him. "You're saying this to a man who hasn't been on a date since he wife died. I totally think it is half-empty."

She laughed again. "You've got a point."

Hunter was intrigued by how different Stacey was tonight – like she was open to the possibility of them. Yesterday, she was nearly impervious, but now, she was graceful and kind. It was as if he was getting a glimpse of a different person, maybe the person she used to be before her husband's accident.

***

Mediterranean Nights was packed. All tables were full with the exception of one near the window facing the street, reserved just for them. Hunter had made sure to ask for that particular seating arrangement to pay homage to their date the day before.

After ordering an exceptional bottle of wine, the two sat at the candlelit table getting to know each other. However, Hunter quietly had to remind himself to focus not on the shape of her lips or the cut of her dress but on her words.

"I have to admit that this feels...strange," Stacey said, putting her black napkin on her lap. "I don't even know how to behave on a date." Her chuckle further expressed her nervousness. "What about you?" She looked up into his green eyes. He seemed distant. "Are you alright?"

Hunter snapped out of his daze. "Huh? Oh, yeah. I'm fine." He cleared his throat. "I just...well...I guess that this is sort of weird for me too. I just..." He stopped mid-sentence, realizing that he was making a fool of himself. "Let me start over," Hunter said, sipping his wine. "I go to the gym, go to the office, go shopping...do the boring stuff. But I don't date. It's too difficult still."

"Yeah, me too." Stacey smiled. "I guess my idea of a good night has changed since I've been alone." She looked across the aisle at a couple, who leaned in to kiss each other. *Get a room*, she thought to herself as she turned back to Hunter.

"What is your idea of a good night?" he asked, interested to know what she truly liked.

"I don't know. I spend so much time by myself until when I think of a relaxing evening it involves a hot dog on the pier and a beer. It's not this." She fidgeted with her napkin and tried to seem up beat.

Hunter chuckled under his breath. They were so in-tune with each other until it was almost scary. "My sentiments exactly. I mean, if I could choose the perfect date it would include jeans, relaxation and just being away from people. I see *people* all day. That's all I do, in fact. It's how I pay my bills."

"So what are we doing here?" she asked in a whisper.

Hunter pushed his glass away from him and sat back in his seat. He looked around at all the couples, who seemed to be just fine in the restaurant, and realized that this was not where they should be. "Do you wanna leave...wanna go?" He motioned towards the door.

Stacey leaned into him with bright eyes. "Would it be rude?"

"Rude? No." He shook his head. He watched her lips for a moment then he smiled. "This is our date, right? We can do want we want to do."

"Alright." She took a deep breath. "Let's go."

Chapter Four

After a quick change of clothes into jeans that fit snuggly around her curved hips and a t-shirt that felt nice against her skin, Stacey hurried out into the night air with Hunter, who only took off his tie and rolled up the sleeves to his oxford.

They headed out on foot towards the pier with one thing in mind. A great late evening snack and cold beer on the Puget Sound. Walking close together down Alki Beach, food-in-hand, they enjoyed the quietness of their temporary existence together.

The wind beat against their bodies as they took in the smell of fresh, moist air and Spuds, the fish and chips diner across the way. Cars past by blasting music and couples walked past them as they slowly strolled.

However, Stacey didn't mind their slowness. She enjoyed watching Hunter and talking to him. Maybe it was because she had been secluded for so long, or maybe it was because he was genuinely a good guy, but she was drawn to him like a moth to a fire.

Even if it was just temporary, Hunter illuminated her world with warmth. *Though he had no idea of the fact.* It was his calm and collective nature and his ability not to take himself too seriously that she admired. Far too many people took themselves too seriously, and it blocked them from their ability to appreciate life. She knew. She was one of them for many years.

Hunter shoved the last of his hotdog into his mouth and wiped his hands on his jeans. "Now, this is my idea of a date," he said, nodding his head with a mouth full of food. "How about you?"

"Oh, yeah," she said, looking up at him. "Simplicity." She exhaled a breath.

"Absolute simplicity," he answered, understanding exactly how she felt. He looked down into her brown eyes and felt lost again. "I don't understand it."

"Understand what?" she asked.

"Why you're single? I mean," he shrugged, "you're beautiful and smart and successful. *Love Knocks* obviously rocks."

"So you read up on me?" Stacey was honored though she had learned long ago to cloak all compliments with humility.

"Of course, I read up on you." He cracked a smile. "You've done quite well for yourself. You're the most sought after author out there- mostly because of your desire to stay away from the very people who keep you wealthy."

"I wouldn't call it wealthy," she said in a huff. "I'm well off. I mean, I don't worry about bills." Stacey knew before she said the words that it was a lie. She was a millionaire several times over.

Normally even the discussion of money would have put her off. However, she knew Hunter had his own. So, it wasn't such a big deal.

"Is that why you keep this up?" he asked, completely oblivious to her concern.

Stacey paused. "Keep what up?"

"The whole *not driving, not traveling outside of Seattle, not allowing certain interviews* thing?" He kicked a rock in their path.

Stacey rolled her eyes in defiance. This wasn't the first time that she had been accused of such a thing. "No. It's no charade, Hunter. I'm really fucked up."

Hunter stopped walking. *Fucked up* was a bit harsh. Traumatized may have been a better explanation for her actions. He looked down at her and grabbed her small hand. There was the sincerest look in her eyes, as if what she was saying was the gospel in some sick, twisted way. Suddenly, he wanted to protect her, but how could he protect her from herself?

Stacey looked away from him. Having been alone so long, she had learned to accept what she had become. A hermit. A pessimist in some ways. A fragment. A fraction of what she used to be.

But Hunter seemed to see something different. Maybe it was because he too had been forever altered by his experience. "You're not fucked up," he finally said, his deep baritone voiced determined.

Stacey smiled. "Of course, I am."

"No, you're not. You're just in a different place right now. We all go through it. I'm going through it," he said, holding both his hand and hers up to his racing heart.

"You're sweet, Hunter. But let's face facts. I own a perfectly good Mercedes that I've only driven once. When I got into it, I totally freaked. I became incredibly claustrophobic all of a sudden. Then, I had a panic attack that nearly killed another family right in a major intersection. It was horrific...no it was pathetic." She yanked her hand away.

They both began to walk again in silence. Hunter thought of all the many changes he'd made in his own life and how difficult things had been for him. He also thought about how difficult he had made things for everyone else- for his family, for what friends were left.

As a surge of foamy waves hit the bay, he gazed over at the water and pushed his own pain aside. How could he help her if he was still groveling? "A Mercedes, you say?"

Stacey took a sip of her Red Stripe beer. "Black-on-black interior. It's a beautiful piece of engineering. I keep it in the parking garage. It has like twenty miles on it."

He chuckled. "You *are* a baller. What do you do with all of that money?"

"Send some home to take care of dad and save the rest," she answered without thought. "What do you do with yours?"

"I send a lot of it to Soldier's Angels. It's an organization that helps military families in need. The rest I save. I'm not really into the whole *living above my means* deal."

"Me either," she said, taking another swig of her beer. "It's totally played out. Taxes make me want to save every penny."

He laughed. "Yeah, the IRS is a bitch."

"Tell me about it," she laughed. "Don't you wish that you could claim someone, be married to someone?"

"All the time," he said in a huff. Both the question and the answer had two meanings for him, but he would keep that to himself.

And just like that, they had moved on from the moment of despair. They walked and laughed for nearly an hour, taking in the sights and the sounds of the boats and waves. Peacefully, they found themselves truly getting to know one another.

Hunter liked to collect Greek artifacts when he wasn't helping run the family practice. He spent a considerable amount of time at the gym and was a horrible golfer and basketball player. Stacey enjoyed collecting old books, buying art from a dealer in Harlem who knew exactly what pieces spoke to her difficult but beautiful childhood. When she wasn't writing, she enjoyed biking and long walks around the waterway. Both had a thing for the Food Network and YouTube. They even were subscribers to some of the same channels.

"Are you on Facebook?" Hunter asked as they sat atop a rock on the bay.

"Oh, yeah. That's how I interact with most of my readers," Stacey said, skipping a rock.

"Yeah, I like Facebook too. I keep in touch with *her* family on it." He perked up. "Are you an HBO freak or a Showtimer?"

"Both," she answered quickly. "I can't live without *Game of Thrones* or *Gigolos*."

Hunter laughed aloud. "I actually record *Game of Thrones*."

Stacey turned to him. The moonlight shone down on her angelic face. With her lips twisted up, she smiled. "We're sort of boring, aren't we?"

Hunter shook his head. "Completely."

"When I write, I never write about people like us. And it's weird, you know, because this is what I know best. I always write about these amazing romances that make your heart beat fast and your blood race. I write just the most incredible love scenes that defy the very existence of real, human relationships." She walked towards him as he sat perched a few feet away on a rock watching her. "I used to live an amazing life, have earth-shattering sex, and have that whole cloud-nine feeling. Did you?"

Hunter shook his head. "Yep."

"I'm sorry. I know that we are supposed to be doing this help each other, but am I becoming too *intimate*?" she paused.

"No. It's just been a long time since anyone else articulated the same emotions that I've had. I tried the counseling and the specialized psychiatrist." Hunter looked up at her. "Nothing worked."

"So did I," Stacey said absently.

"I still don't sleep well. I still don't do a lot of things *well*. After her death, I just wanted to be alone. You know?"

"I know." Stacey sat down beside him. He scooted over to give her room. "Did you try valium?"

"For a while. It made me feel less like myself. I felt like I was cheating. After all, she was dead. So, I felt that mourning was my way of at least feeling something."

"That was my exact thought too." Stacey liked the idea that he didn't hold back. Maybe she didn't have to either. "Can I ask you a totally personal question, since you are a doctor and a widow?" A naughty grin crossed her lips.

He looked over at her and smiled back. "Sure. Why not." *You can ask me anything you want*, he thought to himself.

"Did you lose your desire to...masturbate?"

Hunter frowned. That was not what he was expecting. He chuckled under his breath as she followed his face for an answer. She evidently did not see anything wrong with the question.

"It's odd that you bring that up. Yes, I did." He laughed but still felt odd. *How did she know that?* "It took a year to even think about it. It made me feel like I was cheating on her." He looked down at his crotch involuntarily.

"Me too," she said, slumping over. "It made me grumpier. I bought a drawer full of dildos from Switzerland. They are supposed to have the best *plastics*. At first, I just thought I was buying the wrong type, and then I realized that it was me. I lost the ability to get off."

Hunter was speechless. Never had a woman, even at his practice, shared that with him before. "You're right. We *are* fucked up."

"Tell me about it," she said, raising her beer to his. "To two months together."

"To two months," he said, clinking his beer against hers.

The moon lit her face just right at that very moment. Her long, swan neck ran down to her perfectly toned body, and she appeared to be glowing. He swallowed hard at the thought that she might actually let him kiss her tonight.

Perched on the rocks and drinking beer, they talked until the clouds came and hid the moon behind their thick dark blankets. The smell of rain was the only thing that pulled them from their deep conversations on life, politics, relationship and even children. It had been years since they had opened up so much to anyone, so long since some- one else could identify with their tribulations.

As Hunter watched Stacey explain the beauty of completing a novel, he began to feel worried. Had they opened Pandora's Box? Would they be able to close it? Maybe it was the knowledge that in two months, they would both walk away from this experience and be better for it. Maybe it was because they knew that nothing would be lost. But something was happening tonight between the two of them, and it was strong – strong enough to scare him. However, he was unable to stop himself or his curiosity. With every secret that they shared, somehow he felt better, more alive. Stacey was changing him.

"What about you?" she asked, oblivious to his thoughts. "What makes you happiest about your career?" Rubbing her hands on her jeans, she put down her bottle.

"Saving lives," he said sincerely. He looked up in the night sky. "I've saved six women from ovarian cancer, saved countless more from the misery of discomfort and sickness. It makes me feel good inside."

"I'm sure," Stacey said, proud for him. "That has to be an unbelievable feeling. You know, when my mom died of ovarian cancer, it scared the shit out of me. I wondered how I would recover from her loss. When I did start to have sex, I got checked more than any other girl I know. It was because I had felt so helpless with her situation, and I never wanted to feel that way again. And look at you. You save lives every day. That's amazing. I mean, I've never saved anyone before. The feeling must be unimaginable."

Hunter felt quite the opposite. For just one evening, without knowing it, she was saving him from the boredom that they fondly spoke of.

As a light drizzle of rain began, Stacey and Hunter headed back to her apartment. With every block, Hunter felt a tightness in his chest. He wanted more time with her. Their next date was scheduled for next week. Doubting he could wait that long, he sifted through his schedule in his mind. Who could he cancel? What could he do to see her sooner?

Stacey walked closer than before to him. In stride with each other, she reached out her hand and slid into his strong embrace. There was something about him that seemed familiar. *And nothing felt familiar about men anymore.* Ever since Drew passed, she felt alone in the world, like no one understood her. But Hunter did.

He looked down as he took her hand in his own. Her warm lingers felt good. Squeezing her lightly, he pulled it up to his mouth and kissed it.

"You're a good man, Hunter," she said softly.

The lyrical tone of her voice sounded like music to his ears. It had been a long time since a woman had given him such a kind yet sincere compliment.

The rain began to pour heavily when they arrived at her apartment. Unlocking the door, she almost invited him in. *Almost.* Opening the door, she turned, looked up into his jewel green eyes, fluttering under heavy, tired lashes and sighed.

"Thanks for tonight," she said, coming to grips with the fact that it had to end.

"No, thank you," he said, stepping closer. "Look, I know that we said that we'd do this once a week, but I was really hoping that I could see you tomorrow." He waited.

Stacey shrugged in a tiny, delicate motion that drew attention to the slim column of her neck. "I have to write most of the day, but we could catch dinner afterwards, if you like."

"That sounds nice," he said, inching closer.

"Jeans and t-shirt type of dinner?" she asked, her voice cracked.

"Definitely." His voice was lower now, even more seductive.

Unable to help himself, Hunter lifted her delicate chin up and cupped her oval face in his hands. How beautiful she was. What a sight to behold. Her brown smooth skin felt like satin, hot and alive, perfectly toned like the rest of her, free of blemishes, full of youth.

Running his thumb over her face, he was able to admire even closer the perfect shape of her nose, her high cheek bones and her heart-shaped mouth. A small and tempting mole was right above her velvety, plump and pouty lips. Big brown eyes stared up at him, covered by dense black lashes, speaking to him with their eager curiosity. Stacey Lane Bryant was a work of art, fit to be painted, to be written about, to be loved.

His breath washed against her face as he drew closer. He could feel her body shaking, trembling under his very touch. Her eyes danced with excitement, her warm mouth parted, ready for a kiss. How could he disappoint her? How could he disappoint himself?

His mouth met hers with a soft kiss first, tasting the sweetness on her wet and inviting lips. But as his hands moved to the back of her head and tangled into her long dreadlocks, their embrace became more passionate.

Pushing against her firm breasts, he snaked comfortably around her, shielding her body from view with his large frame. The euphoria of being in a woman's embrace ignited a fire inside of him. He had missed this about life. He had missed what it was like to hold a woman, to enjoy her company, to bask in her beauty.

Fervently, she kissed him back, moaning a little as she fell into him and let her hands run over his concrete chest. Sucking on his bottom lip, she felt her body quake as his delicious tongue mingled with her own.

They kissed for several minutes, forgetting where they were or how long they had been there. It was as if they were making love as sensual sensations filled them both to the brim. Having denied themselves this blessed experience for so long, it was hard to stop, and they knew it would be even more impossible to recover.

Finally, as the heat began to rush in places that Hunter knew would be inappropriate for tonight, he pulled away regretfully from her embrace.

Opening her eyes and resting off her tip toes, Stacey looked up at him amazed. No one had ever kissed her like that, or maybe it had been so long until she could not remember anymore what a kiss even felt like. But one thing was for sure, she did not want to ever forget again.

"Tomorrow for sure," she said, leaning against the door.

"I cannot wait," he said, licking his lips. "I better go." He stepped away from her. "Good night."

Stacey smiled. "Good night, Hunter."

Chapter Five

After Hunter left the night before, Stacey sat in front of her computer in her purple pajamas with a glass of white wine and typed feverishly for many hours until her eyes would not stay open. The characters had changed in her mind. The conversations. The plot. It all took on new life so much so that she ended up changing the entire premise of the novel.

When she finally awoke the next morning, she was still in front of her computer with her head buried in her hands on her desk. Her neck felt like it had a hundred kinks in it, but she was so grateful for the inspiration until she would not complain.

Dragging herself to the kitchen, she made a pot of hazelnut coffee and went out on the balcony to take in the fresh air. The crisp dawn felt good to her skin. And the sky was blessedly clear, like God was rewarding her for trying again. As the winds blew past her, she closed her eyes and smiled.

She could not believe it. Hunter's plan was working, at least for her. Passion. Love. Excitement. Things that had long burned out in her mind were now undeniably present. And it had all started with his marvelous kiss.

His full lips flashed through her mind again for the hundredth time. His precious kiss had tasted so sweet, so full of virility. It made her think of what he must be like in bed. *He* made her think of sex.

Their agreement was still iron-clad as far as she was concerned. However, he made it harder for her to stick by with his strong capable hands that had searched her neck while he kissed her, embraced her body and aroused her to her soul.

***

Hunter kept looking at his watch as he sat in his office reading over Mrs. Clementine's file. Why did it seem that today of all days, the time wanted to inch by? Frustrated, he took the pen from the pocket of his smock and wrote something down then closed the manila folder and pushed it away from him.

"Something the matter?" his sister asked, coming into the office behind him.

Hunter looked up and straightened in his seat. "No. I just have something to do tonight."

"*Something to do?*" she asked curiously. "Does it involve a woman?"

Hunter smiled and stuck the pen behind his ear. "Yes, as a matter of fact, it does." The thought of Stacey made him smile.

"Well, I'll be damned. Who is she? Someone I know?" Hanna asked, grabbing a seat.

"You could say that. She's a patient."

Hanna was suddenly quiet as ethical issues crossed her mind. "Did you see her?"

"No. Well, I almost did, but then I referred her to you. Stacey Bryant. She came in the other day as a new patient."

Hanna frowned. It was surely not who she thought it was. "The black woman?" she asked.

"Yes, *the black woman*," Hunter said, shaking his head. *Leave it to her to make that an issue.* He had not gone on a date or seen a woman in two years, and the only thing that she could focus on was the color of her skin.

"I didn't mean it that way. You've just never dated anyone who wasn't Greek," she said defensively.

Hanna could instantly feel his resistance to her statement. She countered with a fake smile, trying to cover her hesitation. Maybe this was simply his way of moving back into the dating scene. Having known him all of her life, she recognized the frown lines in his perfectly tanned skin and tried to retract her statement. After all that he had gone through, the last thing that she wanted to do was discourage him.

Hunter could not deny his sister a pardon. "Stacey and I have a mutual understanding. She lost her husband a few years ago, too. We just both need someone right now. I can't expect you to understand completely. You've got Jack. But I'm getting older and even lonelier. Some part of me needs this." His voice was solemn.

Hanna and Hunter were two years apart in age with Hunter being the oldest. The two had a very close relationship. They had gone to college together, defied their parents together and so much more. Out of the four children of their family, the two were the closest. In fact, she had mourned for Corina nearly as hard as her brother.

After all, they had all three been friends. It was because of their connection that she had always been so protective over him. Maybe too protective.

"Well, if she's what you need right now, I fully support you," she lied. "Let's just keep this from Mom and Dad."

Hunter rolled his eyes. "You know, I never realized that we were prejudice until right now." His finger pointed down on the table.

One of the nurses walked past their door and politely closed it shut. Evidently, their conversation was floating into the rest of the clinic, which could potentially be b*ad for business.* Both of them looked over at the door and moaned.

"We're not prejudice, Hunter. Dad is just pro-Greek," Hanna explained, wishing that she had never broached the subject. It was not her business anyway.

"Right," Hunter said, standing up. "I've got work to do. Just do me a favor, will you? Let me decide what is best for me. I know how you are and how you like to interject your own opinions in my life. In the past, some of the time, it was helpful. But I doubt with this particular situation that you could offer any useful insight."

Opening the door, he looked over at her one last time and made a motion over his lips like he was zipping them.

***

Valerie was absolutely ecstatic. Holding the pages that she had printed of Stacey's latest story, she paced from side-to-side of her Manhattan office and sang her praises.

"It is truly your best work yet, Stacey," Valerie said, stopping at her desk to put the manuscript down.

"You think?" Stacey asked, writing notes on her notepad while they talked on speakerphone.

"I know so. However, I wasn't expecting an interracial twist. That is something new."

"My readers could be disappointed. I know, but right now, that is just the direction that I'm going."

"Well, truthfully, African-American women are reading more and more interracial novels. And many are dating outside of their race. You're just keeping up with the times. It's damned near mainstream," Valerie said, trying not to upset Stacey. If it was a problem later, they would handle it when they got to it. For now, she didn't foresee anything but seven-figure dollar signs.

"Great," Stacey answered, releasing a heavy sigh of relief.

"So where did your motivation come from? Anyone in particular?" Valerie held the phone. Could it be that Stacey had turned in her hermit card? She hoped so. The two had been friends, *sort of*, for a few years, and since Drew's death, she had witnessed Stacey nearly give up on life.

Stacey laughed. "Let's just say that I took your advice."

"His name?"

"Hunter," Stacey answered quickly.

"His profession?"

"Doctor." She sounded proud, as if she had picked the cream of the crop.

"Wow, I'm impressed." Valerie waved in her assistant and looked at her watch. It was time to call to another author. *Time was money, friend or not.* "So we're still on schedule then?"

"Absolutely," Stacey said, knowing what the pause in Val's voice meant.

"Wonderful. Well, I'll talk to you soon, doll. Be good. I can't wait to read the rest of this amazing story. It's a hit!"

"Thanks," Stacey said, hanging up the phone.

Rapture was there by Stacey's side as soon as the line went dead, begging for her complete attention. Picking him up, she tucked him into her embrace and looked at her computer screen full of words that only days ago were not imaginable. She felt as if she could type all the rest of the evening, but she had to get ready for her date.

Her cat could feel her sudden detachment and purred for her attention. Nudging his head under her neck, he begged for a hug.

"I still love you, kitty," Stacey said, feeling his sadness.

However, Stacey was even more excited about seeing Hunter than Valerie was about receiving her new manuscript. All day long the wheels in her head had been turning, not only about her story, but also about tonight. She felt high on life. It was almost scary. If it weren't for their arrangement, she might have boxed up her emotions and ran, but at least now, she was safeguarded in some way from a broken heart...hopefully.

***

Hunter hit the gym harder than normal. He had to do something to rid himself of the sexual frustration that seemed to be ripping into his every thought.

One would have imagined, considering his profession, that the female form would be old to him by now, less exhilarating, less exciting, and before Stacey, it had been. But the taste of her lips the night before had awakened him and the beast inside of his cob-webbed libido.

Pushing the speed button on the treadmill, he accelerated his run. Faster, Harder. Stronger. He needed more of everything. Sweat poured down his face and neck onto his gray t-shirt. His calf muscles burned and his arms tightened. Maybe if he exhausted himself physically, he would be too tired tonight to think of every inch of Stacey's body. Plus, it would be much harder to control his desires while on their date if he did not take matters into his own hands...literally.

A thought about Stacey trying to masturbate unsuccessfully crossed his mind, and he laughed aloud.

The woman beside Hunter looked over at him curiously.

"Sorry," he said, turning up his MP3 player.

Their arrangement was going to be harder than he had originally thought. True, he had been attracted to her since the moment that he laid eyes on her, but he had never imagined that she would taste so sweet, smell so fragrant, feel so good under his fingertips.

How long had it been? Forever. Sex had become a thought of what *used* to be in his life – when he had one. There had not been one other woman since his wife died. In the past, old girlfriends called and dropped by without notice to try to *comfort* him. Colleagues offered it at conferences like it was candy. Random, nameless women suggested it every time that he was at the bar, but no matter who it was, there was a wall blocking him from exploring what sex would be like with another woman.

Now the thoughts that had been suppressed due the trauma of his wife's sudden passing were back and if possible, stronger. And they were leading him around like he was a lost puppy dog.

Nevertheless, he had to remember himself with Stacey, because she obviously trusted him more than he trusted himself. The way that she shared the most intimate details of her life let him know that she was unsure of how to function in the dating scene, just like him. With their significant others, they had been open books, and after they had died, both he and Stacey had completely shut down. Now that they were trying to open up again, even if for just a while, there would be little room for games or lies.

Chapter Six

Stacey had never enjoyed kissing a man so much. Leaning against his chest, as they watched television on her couch, she felt completely safe in his embrace. A quiet, Sunday afternoon passed as they sat cuddled up together by the fireplace and quizzed each other on the Brat pack. The *Breakfast Club* played on the television as they watched each other and reminisced about the 80's.

Under heavy lashes, Hunter went in and out of consciousness after half a bottle of wine and a bowl of extra greasy buttered popcorn.

"Am I too heavy?" Stacey asked, placing her hand on the side of the sofa to push herself up.

Hunter's eyes flashed open as she tried to move. Grabbing her waist, he pulled her back down on him. "No, you're as light as a feather," he said, opening his legs to push her down in between them. "Don't go." His voice was tranquil and content.

Smiling, she snuggled back down between his legs and hummed, happy as a lark. They both wore their college t-shirts and gray cotton jogging pants, which added to their lazy day comfort. His bare feet rubbed against Rapture, who had settled down at the end of the couch near them.

Resting her head back down on his chest, she moved in to kiss his full mouth again. "I've never liked kissing this much in my life," she admitted, tasting his bottom lip.

"Me either," he said, rubbing her sandy brown dreads.

"Umm...But I need to get up and wash my hair."

"Let me do it for you," he said, kissing her forehead.

"Do you want to?" she asked, a little excited about having someone pamper her for a change.

"Of course. Your hair is so different from mine. It feels like...I don't know...bushels of cotton. But the smell is intoxicating like you put an entire bouquet of roses in it."

"I wash it with jasmine shampoo," she whispered. "It's to draw you in more."

"It's working." Hunter looked at her and ran his hand over the plains of her face. "Stacey, I can truly say that I haven't been this happy in a long time." His deep baritone shook in nervousness. "Thank you for doing this...for agreeing to be my friend."

Stacey blushed at his sincerity, although she felt like they were more than friends. A wrinkle formed across her forehead as her voice lowered. "We are more than that aren't we?"

Hunter smiled. "Yeah but I don't really know how to classify what we are. Do you? I mean, I don't kiss my friends like this. I don't want to spend every waken moment that I'm not working with *my friends*."

"Speaking of friends, I don't know any of yours, and I don't have any. We are a strange couple."

Hunter ran his hand over her backside. "Well, I told you about Piper and John. They are my closest friends. Maybe we could go to dinner with them soon. I'd like for you to meet them."

"Do you think that's a good idea, considering our arrangement?"

Hunter sat up. "I've been meaning to talk to you about that."

Stacey rose up with him. Sitting on her knees in between his legs, she grabbed Rapture and held him in her arms as a defense mechanism. What was he about to say? Was this not working for him anymore? Had he met someone else? It had been a glorious month, but still a month with no sex. Maybe he was growing tired of their arrangement.

Hunter grabbed the remote to turn off the television as Emilio Estevez was right in the middle of the famous dance scene. He turned to Stacey, took Rapture and put him on the floor and grabbed her hand. Her long, brown fingers, perfectly shaped with long, curved fingernails, rested in his own.

"This started out as an experiment, a way to get over Drew and Corina, but for me, it has grown into something more. I don't want just two and a half months with you." He looked down at her hands, trembling in his own. "Please tell me that it has changed for you, too. If it hasn't then I understand, because we are all entitled to our own feelings but..."

"Hunter..." Stacey could feel her entire body shaking apart. "I have felt like that since we kissed the first night." She decided to tell the truth. Shame the devil.

"Really?" Hunter gave a bright triumphant smile.

"Yes, I just didn't want to be the first one to jump, for lack of a better word." The answering looking her vulnerable brown eyes was melting. "I'm a hopeless romantic. Otherwise, I'd be a lousy author, not to say that I'm the best now."

"You're amazing. I read your last book. I can see why you're a bestselling author."

"You are just a tiny bit biased," she said, putting her index finger and thumb together.

"Okay, maybe I am, but you're brilliant, and you know it. The whole world knows it."

She smiled. "Flattery will get you everywhere."

"Be my girl?" he asked, pulling her to him. He had waited long enough to ask. A month was torture to be around her and not have her for sure.

She crawled up in his embrace. "Only if you promise to still take it slow."

Hunter couldn't promise that. For 30 days, he had tried every trick in the book to keep his physical feelings at bay. But for her sake, he lied. "As slow as you want," he said, lifting her chin up to see her face. "There is still no pressure, there never will be."

"Okay," she whispered. "We can try this thing out on a more permanent basis."

The relief of her decision was now evident in his bright eyes. A deep sigh escaped him and within seconds his hands went everywhere defying his own promise to take it slow.

Ravaging her mouth, he sank back down into her leather sofa, taking her with him as he did. He felt like a high school kid again, fighting to keep his control. Her smell, the softness of her lips, the heavy weight of her dreads in his hands, the warm feeling of her body against his, made the heat in his body rise to a volcanic temperature.

Stacey was almost alarmed by his passion. *Was this his idea of taking things slow?* Unable to fight his kiss, she fell on top of him, holding on to his muscular shoulders as she suddenly felt his erection prodding just above her navel. Her natural instinct prohibited her from pulling away. She was amazed at the hard, thickness below. An ache began to fill her lower belly right before the sensation landed squarely between her steaming thighs.

"We had better get to washing my hair," she said, finally as she realized that for the first time in a long time, she was wet...unforgivably soaking wet.

Flush red, he looked up at her and calmed himself. His hot hands ran over his stubbly beard. "Sorry," he whispered with a naughty grin. He looked into her eyes and almost suggested what they both were clearly thinking but was afraid of the possibility of her turning him down and worse shutting down.

Rapture sat on the floor looking at both of them with his silver eyes flickering in the dim room. The tilt of his little head suggested that he too was confused or maybe intrigued by their odd pairing.

Hunter looked over at the cat and raised his brow. "I bet you weren't ready for that one," he said to Rapture as Stacey got up and went to the bathroom.

"Do you wash your hair naked?" he yelled as he heard the water running. He could hear her laughing. "Just a thought," he said under his breath as he sat up.

Slowly walking through the apartment with the cat trailing at his feet, he entered into her bedroom and looked around. It was warm and welcoming like the rest of her home.

The walls were painted in a deep purple with one wall of exposed brick. Two large windows with heavy plum, expensive curtains faced the bay. One very large elegant bed sat in the middle of the room, perfectly made, with a plum colored comforter and large pillows. Hunter stared at it for a minute intrigued. It was the only thing in her house that didn't fit. It was a great deal more ornate and luxurious than anything else she owned.

On each side of the bed were wooden nightstands and clear acrylic lamps with beige shades. By each lamp was a stack of books and bouquet of roses. The walls were adorned more black framed art and in the corner was an antique wooden rocking chair with a beige pillow and beige throw cover.

A thought crossed his mind, but he quickly shut it out. There was no need to dwell on things that he could not have.

What he did notice was that in the perfect little room she did not have a television. He knew instantly that because of her inability to sleep, her shrink, *like his*, had suggested no TV. However, unlike him, she'd actually listened. He, on the other hand, had purchased a 60-inch plasma and had it installed on the wall right across from his bed.

On the wall across from her bed was an antique large dresser, embroidered with intricate designs. On top of it was a picture of who must have been her father and her as a child sitting on a stoop outside of a brownstone. The other picture, framed in silver, was a picture of Drew.

He was a handsome, clean shaven black man with eyes the color of hazelnut and prominent ethnic features. His smile suggested that he was happy, *but who wouldn't be with Stacey*. She had told Hunter once that Drew was an astrophysicist. Her story humbled him. All this time, he had thought he ran in *intelligent* circles, while this guy was studying Mars.

Hearing the water running in the bathroom, he turned and looked at the room again in one final assessment. Stacey was neat, simple and classy. He liked that about her. She was worth millions but her conservative spending and her less than gaudy personality only required comfort. Any man who lived in this society could appreciate a woman who had pulled herself up by her own bootstraps and still was grounded, *rooted was a better word for Stacey*.

Hunter had considered dating a few times before, but everyone that his family and friends had tried to hook him up with was so centered on appearance and prestige until it made him sick. While he was a doctor with a thriving practice, he just wanted to be a guy with a comfortable life. This was why he had settled on a nice condo in a nice part of town but not anything that would break the bank.

Overall, it was hard to find a woman, regardless of color, who wanted the same types of things in life that he wanted, because what he wanted most was simplicity. Strangely enough, he had found it in Stacey. She was clever, always saying things that stuck with him long after their conversation had ended. She was inquisitive about even the smallest parts of his life, and she was sure of herself.

In the four weeks that he'd known her, the one thing that he had learned to appreciate most about her was that she was sincere. She had no ambitions to conquer the world or to be the most known or most sought after, even though by some measure she had conquered her world and was highly regarded. How many women could say that? For that matter, how many men knew a woman who was doing that? He felt honored.

"I'm waiting, Hunter," she said, turning the water off in her tub. "Are you going to do this or should I?" Her voice was playful.

"No, I'm coming. You know, I've never really seen your bedroom before. It's nice."

"Thanks," she said, sounding a bit preoccupied. "No, Rapture. Go," she ordered. Her voice echoed in the bathroom.

Scratching the back of his tousled hair, Hunter rounded the corner and paused. His eyes widened at the sight before him. Stacey was sitting in her white garden tub full of crimson rose petals naked with her dreads down covering the brown tips of her perky breasts.

"I hope that there is nothing wrong with a little spontaneity," she said, waving her hands in the water. Her eyes begged for his approval. Trying to still her quivering voice, she reached out for him. "We can take things *slowish* later."

Walking up to the tub, Hunter looked down at her body and licked his lips. His eyes were wild with lusty thoughts. Greedily taking in her body, he studied her in amazement. Her skin was perfect. Warm brown flesh unblemished and toned sat atop of lean muscle and continuous curves. Her bright brown eyes spoke of passion and desire that he had never truly seen before in her.

"Did I move to fast?" she asked suddenly, preparing to draw back into her shell.

Hunter realized in that moment that he had not uttered a word. He stammered. "No...you just look...I never imagined that you were so beautiful."

She blushed, showing a deceiving innocence. "Thank you." Picking up the shampoo, she passed it to him.

"You're killing me," he said jokingly. "You still want me to wash your hair?"

"Yes," she laughed. "Play along. You'll be rewarded."

Her banter made him hard. Quickly, he opened the top and dropped a blob of shampoo in his hands then sat on the edge of the tub. The cold porcelain did nothing to cool his growing heat. Rubbing the shampoo into her hair, he watched her angelic eyes close. *Ah, now she's enjoying it*, he thought to himself. He massaged her temples then took the ceramic cup and stuck into the water to rinse her off.

As the water cascaded down her long back, he felt his pants rise up with a steely erection. *God, she is so sensual*, he thought to himself as he washed her. His hands trailed down her neck to her narrow shoulders and massaged her tense muscles. He ached to go further and cup her breasts. Rigid and inviting, they waited for him.

Slow, he reminded himself as the water trickled over her face. It was her moan that devoured him. Biting her lip, a deep throaty sound came from within her that stabbed at his most erogenous senses.

"I can't do this," he said, standing up. "Not I can't do this...I mean, I can't do this *like* this." *Don't mess this up*, he berated himself inwardly.

She wiped her face and looked up confused. Had she done something wrong? Was it not time?

Without any more words, Hunter pealed out of his shirt to reveal carved muscle then pulled off his pants and underwear and kicked them across the room.

Stacey's eyes grew with intrigue as she looked over at him. Handsome was not a powerful enough word to describe his statuesque body. She bit her bottom lip as she watched.

"Mind if I get in?" he asked in a deep husky voice, realizing her eyes had settled at his rock hard erection. He ran his large hand over it to add insult to her injury, displaying its unimaginable girth and length.

She shook her head and pushed out the words that seemed to be stuck behind her tongue. "No. There is enough room for you." *I don't know about it*, she thought to herself.

Quickly, he stepped in the warm water and sat down behind her. He sighed in bliss as the water lapped at his hips and waist.

The sensation of skin-on-skin caused goose bumps to form all over her body. Scooting up to give him room, she felt his strong, capable hands, yank her back onto his lap causing the water to splash over her. His heartbeat boomed against her back as he embraced her. Closing her eyes for a moment, she delighted in the feel of him. She wasn't going to allow herself to regret this no matter what happened in their relationship. It had been so long until she needed this, even if he didn't.

Hunter watched her closely from behind. The time for being a gentleman was nearing an end. Holding her arms in his hands, he nuzzled his face into her hair and inhaled her jasmine scent. "Are you ready?" he asked abruptly. His voice was hard and demanding.

"Yes," she hissed with her eyes closed. She had never felt so exquisitely alive.

Bracing herself on his pulsing lap, she touched his large thighs covered in black hair and nestled against his concrete body. Her nails raked his skin and made him clench his jaw tighter. His penis was pushed between them, resting against his stomach and her lower back, but for the moment, he ignored it.

A breath caught in her chest when his hands moved. He felt amazing, better than she had imagined, and he was even more beautiful naked than clothed.

Hunter had an athlete's build, sinewy and detailed, wide and foreboding. His chest stuck out with pounds of hard flesh cut to perfection atop of it and his masculine sandalwood smell was even more intoxicating when there were no clothes to mask it.

Covertly, she took a deep breath to smell him better.

His hands trailed over her hot skin, massaging her body as he calmed her. Her breaths slowed with every touch. Then quietly he went back to washing her.

Taking his time, he studied the kinky long hair in his hand, washing it with great care. He had never had the pleasure of touching hair like hers before. It was exotic and sexy. He didn't know why but it turned him on more.

With her hair soapy, he filled the ceramic cup again and rinsed it, growing harder as the water ran from her head down to her pebbled nipples and further down her stomach past her tiny belly button.

She made matters worse when she ran both of her hands over her breasts and squirmed on top of him. Her full weight was now in his lap, pushing against his most sensitive parts. His mouth grew anxious. He wanted nothing more than to have one of those chocolate morsels in the mouth to bite and suck.

Unable to control himself, he pulled her head to him and kissed her wet neck. His lips felt like silk against her. She moaned, breaths picking up again in excitement.

"You're so beautiful," he whispered into her ear before he bit it.

Intoxicated, she reached back and wove her long finger into his thick black hair. As her arms lifted, her breasts were in better view. He had never seen a better pair.

Undulating under her, he clenched his square jaw as tight as he could. He knew that he should have a condom on, but there was no way in hell that he was getting out of this tub. Plus, he had secretly read her file. She was clean, nothing to worry about but impregnating her. Besides at the present his chaotic mind didn't think that was such a bad idea. In fact, the idea strangely turned him on more.

He ran his hands down her back as she leaned forward, and he massaged her tiny waist. Her skin was like wet satin against his fingertips. Cupping her buttocks, he raised her up and let his middle finger slip inside of her delicate folds.

"Ahh," she called out. "Yes, Hunter. Yes."

Warm and wet, she moved against him. Her sex stretched a little, tight from years of abstinence. That seemed to turn him on more. She was such a good woman, a patient woman, a beautiful creature. The primitive part of his brain regarded her with complete and total possessiveness. She belonged to him now. All of her. *This is mine*, he thought to himself as he stuck another finger inside of her. She moaned again - the pleasure of his strokes evident on her stunning face.

The sound of water splashing mixed with her soft, feminine moans and the dimness of the room in candlelight entranced him. Her wet hair slapped against his skin like whips. Her graceful body smacked against him as she moved around turned on past his wildest dreams. He literally had to hold on to her as he fondled her. She was completely turned on, ready to do whatever he wanted.

Rock hard and dying to be inside of her, he replaced his eager fingers with his needy cock. His swollen head pulsed as he entered her. Her wetness slicked her lips even in the water, making his admittance even more paralyzing. Zingers shot through both of them.

She screamed aloud as her body stretched then wrapped tight around his hungry erection. Hard suction swallowed him up into her body and her thighs locked him in for the ride. Stacey threw back her head and arched her back further, screaming out as she looked up to the ceiling. Her sandy dreads felt down between them, cloaking her back. He moved her hair quickly then ran his hand down her spine.

She was darker naked. Parts of her body were as deep brown as molasses and as sweet. He wanted to taste every inch of her. Kissing her shoulder, he felt her adjust herself to his need. He waited patiently before he began his invasion of her body, looking for all the signs to let him know that she was ready. Resting his head back on the back of the tub, he guided her down with his grip. His hands clutched her tiny waist, squeezing her body tight.

"Hunter," she called out as her back arched and her legs positioned themselves to take all of him.

With seriousness in his face, he focused as his hips moved from side to side, wedging his heated flesh into her folds. Suddenly and without warning, the magnificent thrusting began. The water splashed as her body moved up and down against him. She shuddered under his power, feeling the need and heat build within her thighs.

Lifting her and pulling her down, he growled as he watched her submit. Her hands were at first firmly placed to hold herself up, but with each blow to her core, they became weaker. But Hunter was hungry for more than just her backside. He wanted to see her face; he wanted to feel her body against his.

Turning around, she sat on top of him again. He found her breasts quickly, suckling one in between his lips and squeezing the other. Looking into her eyes, he invaded her again, this time slowly when he felt her swollen womb tighten around him.

Her gaze was devastating. Free of lipstick, her wide pouty mouth opened to call his name again, but he quickly found her lips and kissed her. He had never kissed such a full mouth. He had never made love to such dark skin. He had never done a lot of things he was about to do.

Their tongues played back and forth as she straddled him. Years of riding a bike proved an advantage as she held her position. Powerfully, she moved atop of him as he watched in amazement of her sexual transformation.

The fact that she had opened up this far to him was mind-blowing. The fact that she had broken her own rules for him, showed that he had finally earned her trust, but there was more than just trust working here. Since he'd started seeing her, the nightmares were fewer, his mind was more at peace and he knew it all was because of her. Awash with raw emotion and on fire for her, he realized that she had become everything to him.

Cupping her face, in his hands he confessed. "I love you," he whispered against her skin. His eyes flickered in the darkness – the fire behind them ablaze.

Her mouth quivered. "I love you, too," she said as tears began to fall.

They embraced each other tightly, still locked together in their love making. The weight of their actions began to ground them, pull them from the cloud that they had floated up to.

Picking her up out of the water, he carried her soaking wet out to the bed. He had just wondered about what it would be like to make love to her here, now he would find out. The thought pushed him into a sweet euphoria.

Anxiously, she lay against the comforter with soap still on her skin playing with herself as he watched. She was spirited; he'd give her that, and for the first time, he could see all of her. Her long legs were carved to perfection. Wide hips, tight muscles, impeccable calves, perfect feet. He ran his hands over her in amazement. Her stomach was lined with muscle, her toned arms powerful from riding her bike, her breasts sat up perky, full and inviting. And her vagina was pampered and clean shaven, shaped into a heavenly v. It was the most beautiful vagina that he'd ever seen, *and he was a doctor.*

Looking up at him, she opened her arms to receive him as he fell into her embrace again. The ceiling fan above chilled their skin as they kissed. Rolling around in the bed, they explored each other's bodies as they went from one position to the next.

He was amazed with her agility and how she seemed to like sex. It had been his experience that many women did not, either because the man was inexperienced or the woman had no penchant for it. However, his Stacey was wild with desire. And now that she had let her guard down, she had no problem showing how much she liked it.

Laughing, she threw her head back as he nestled his face in her breasts. Her giggle made him smile. Throwing her leg over him, she called his name playfully. His hips rolled in a smooth motion between her thighs that sent waves of ecstasy through her trembling body.

This was what he had missed. This was the part of life that he had denied himself, but it was well worth the wait. To be with a woman so in touch with what she wanted, so open, so giving was worth never touching another woman again.

Her waist moved around as she pushed him inside of her, making sure to not leave an inch of his thick, pulsing manhood out of her body. She bit her pouty lips and sucked in a breath as she took him, pumping and prodding at her in every way.

Holding him close, she looked into his eyes and kissed him. She knew also that her own climax was upon them. However, something would not allow them to part.

The heat began to course through his veins, crippling his ability to move. He felt the ache down in his core as he pumped into her. A vein stuck out of his neck as he strained. His seed prepared to push out, but he could not refuse himself the primitive desire that begged louder than his reason. *Take her*, it said to him. *Take her now*.

As she arched her back and screamed, liquid heat exploded through her body. Her supple breasts pointed out and long hair fell down on his legs. Her body shook with great but waning power, and she nearly collapsed on top of him.

Never had anything felt so primitive, so right. He gritted his teeth and grabbed her. Her body shook with the force of his thrusts as he grasped her hips, pulling back to meet each one. He knew then that he should have pulled out, but he did not want to. He pumped harder, faster, gritting his teeth as he let out a loud masculine moan. Into her body, he felt himself rush like a hot wave of white foam on the beach above him. Suddenly he thought of their walk along the Alki and could hear the waves crashing against the earth.

It may have been that she was in ecstasy or that she felt the same as he did, but she did not stop him. Instead, she kissed his mouth and held on to his throbbing body below, extracting every last ounce of him.

After the transfer of everything that they had both physically and emotionally, he looked into her eyes, panting and speechless. *What had he just done and why didn't he care?* He looked at her body attached to his and wondered as he tried to repress a deviant smile.

Tears sprang from her eyes as her mouth quivered. She too had felt the jolt of love and belonging that they both had been denied and had in returned denied themselves finally return after so many years.

Pulling her to him, he hugged her tightly, rubbing her back and whispering soft, calming words in to her ear. He meant them all. *I love you. I'm here. I'm not going anywhere.*

How's that for slowish? he thought to himself as she laid on top of him naked and trembling. It was more like fools rush in, and he and Stacey were first through the finish line.

Chapter Seven

As the fresh Horiatiki salad was passed to her, Hanna sat under the inquisition of her mother and father about her brother and ate her very uncomfortable meal. This was the sixth Sunday that Hunter had not shown up for dinner, leaving her alone with the vultures. And the feeling around the room was divisively ominous. She debated back and forth with her thoughts. Should she tell them all the truth? Their son was neglecting his family, because he was involved in a relationship with a *black* woman. She rolled her eyes. *Absolutely incredible.*

Hunter had been the president of the Young Greeks of Seattle, the prime pick of their social circle from middle school until the day he had married Corina. And their family had even been disapproving of her, a full-bloodied Greek from a lower socio-economic class than the Fourakis family. They expected him to damn near marry royalty. Why they had always been like that, she had no idea, but they were a pretentious clan as were many of their family friends.

For as long as she could remember, Hunter had always been a proud Greek American, always ranting and raving about the permanent contributions that their culture had given to the world. Now, he was seriously dating a woman who by all standards of their family was beneath them. She wondered was he doing this to spite them all or if he had actually fallen for the woman. He claimed that she had something that he needed. Sex? Companionship? Only God knew.

"Is something the matter?" Dr. Fourakis asked his youngest daughter as he sat at the head of the table watching her suspiciously. He had a knack for knowing when something wasn't right with his children, specifically Hanna.

Hanna gave a weak smile and picked up the salad dressing. "No, what would make you say that, Papa?"

"You seem distant," Mrs. Fourakis chimed in. "And where is your brother? You have to know what is going on with the boy. Is he depressed again? You know how he gets during this time of the year. He should really go back to see the therapist. He needs to talk to someone."

Paris, the eldest brother, nodded but did not answer. Mirroring his brother's handsome face with streaks of silver in his hair and even more refinement in his poise, he sat and listened with a keen ear then looked over at his sister, Rhea, a heavier-set image of Hanna, who sat up straight with the wine glass perched to her plum-colored lips.

Paris and Rhea were not the matriarch and patriarch of the family, but it was easy to confuse them with the two. Seasoned doctors of prestige with a long line of *letters* behind their names, over

300 published studies, articles and academic papers between the two of them, they had taken on the role as the eldest of the children with a certain amount of seriousness that could not be easily ignored.

"He's always been far too emotional for my taste," Paris said absently of Hunter.

"He was coddled too much as a child," Rhea reiterated. It had been her argument for years to the family.

"Or not enough." Hanna rolled her eyes. She hated their sanctimonious bull crap. Why would anyone want to come here and visit, only to be ridiculed the entire time?

"And you've always taken up for him far too much," Rhea said with a nasty snarl to Hanna.

"He's becoming a hermit," Dr. Fourakis said in a matter-of-fact tone. "I invited him to help with the festival this year, but he said that he had *things* to do." He said so with a chuckle as if the boy had no life outside of work.

"Honestly, he gets worse each year. You would think that he would want to move on. I met a lovely girl at the church that I wanted to introduce him to, but he won't even consider a date," Mrs. Fourakis said, feeling a tinge of sympathy for her son and the sudden need to take up for him. Hunter had always been different from his siblings and more sensitive.

Hanna shook her head as they talked. They were so off. Huffing, she stabbed her lettuce and looked over at her mother. "He's seeing a woman." Everyone's eyes landed on her as the words came out. A million questions swirled around the room.

"Is she a doctor?" Mrs. Fourakis asked with an inquisitive smile.

"No," Hanna answered.

"Is she a member of the church?" Mrs. Fourakis asked hopefully.

"He doesn't even go anymore, Ma. No," Hanna replied.

Dr. Fourakis frowned and put down his glass of wine. "Is she Greek?" That was the most important of his concerns but not the only one.

"No," Hanna said, raising her brow. "She's an author though."

"Oh," Mrs. Fourakis said pleased. "Published?"

"Yes, a bestselling author," Hanna said, looking at Rhea, who had attempted but failed to accomplish such a thing. It was worth it to leak Hunter's business just to rub Rhea's shortcomings in her smug face.

Everyone seemed interested suddenly. Maybe they had all been too hard on the boy. He was actually trying to move on with his life. It definitely explained his absence, but it only brought more attention to his love interest. Who was she?

"Well, if she isn't Greek then *what* is she?" Dr. Fourakis exploded. He had had enough of the guessing games.

"She's black," Hanna bit out. She looked down at her food. The room became silent. The clink of silverware falling against plates expressed the consensus. Disapproval.

"Black?" Mrs. Fourakis asked, looking around confused.

"Yes, mother. Black. She's a black author. She writes romance, and she's a patient at the practice, though that is not the way that they initially met," Hanna said quickly.

"Completely unprofessional," Rhea said in a huff.

Hanna shot Rhea a dirty look out of the side of her eye. Leave it to Rhea to be disapproving, though she was still lacking a man or any semblance of a stable relationship.

"How *did* they meet?" Dr. Fourakis asked.

"Is this a joke?" Mrs. Fourakis asked with a half-grin. She still had not caught up to the rest of the conversation. She was still focused on her son seeing a black woman.

Hanna was quiet. She looked at her mother and smirked. "He wants us to stay *out* of his business. And it is serious. He hasn't been home in a few days. He comes to the office and then he goes straight to *her* house. And I wasn't supposed to say anything, but it sounded like a better option than you berating him behind his back."

"We weren't berating..." Rhea started to defend.

"You were," Hanna said, picking up her fork.

"A black author? Really?" Paris asked intrigued. "Do you know her name?"

"I've said enough," Hanna said, refusing to say more. "The point is that he's no hermit."

Dr. Fourakis sat back from the table disgusted. Wiping his face off with the white napkin beside him, he stood up with his hands fisted and stomped off from the table leaving his food uneaten. The maid in the corner quickly stepped forward and pushed his seat up to the table then removed his plate.

Mrs. Fourakis sat in shock. Her dear boy was dating a woman and had not bothered to tell her. He was finally in love and had not shared such a marvelous fact. Hurt to her heart, she stood up from the table. "If you'd excuse me, I'm going to go and check on your father," she said, holding her diamond-covered hand to her St. John powder blue jacket.

Paris nodded and patted his wife's hand as she sat quietly listening and eating her food. "Another dinner at the Fourakis house," he said, turning to Hanna. "You and your brother are absolutely amazing. He ruins dinner by not coming, and you ruin dinner by doing the complete opposite."

"The words *pompous* and *prick* ring a bell when I see that grin of yours," Hanna said to Paris.

"Funny," Paris said snidely. "And where is Jack this evening?"

"He's on duty at the ER," Hanna said, narrowing her eyes.

"Right," Paris said, standing up. "Keep telling yourself that, sweetheart."

Chapter Eight

Wednesday was damp and rainy. Looking out of his office window, Hunter fought with his thoughts as he talked into his recorder. Under the sterile fluorescent lights in his office, he paced back and forth trying to decide which birth control would be best for Mrs. Alderman considering her desire to continue smoking. Her unhealthy habit could lead to blood clots or even a heart attack in view of the fact that she was already over thirty-five.

"Oh, good. You're still here," Hanna said, coming into the office. She closed the door behind her. "Can I talk to you for a minute?"

Hunter looked at his watch, hoping that whatever she wanted wouldn't take long. "Sure. What's up?"

"How have you been?" she asked with a small grin. "You've been like a ghost in here. You're in. You're out. I hardly see you." Hanna shrugged as she held his gaze.

Hunter put down his recorder on the table. Something was up. His eye twitched at the thought of what it could be. "Yeah, sorry about that. I've just been a bit busy." He walked over to his desk and turned on his computer monitor.

"Well, you missed the family dinner again, and now everyone is getting worried," she said, trying to sound concerned.

"I'm a grown man, Hanna. I have other things to do with my Sunday's than sit and fight with Paris and Rhea." He went to *Google* and typed something in. Turning his eyes from her, he tried to calm his defenses. It seemed that he had to do that a lot lately with her.

"The family is talking, Hunter. They're worried," Hanna explained in a strained voice.

Hunter stabbed the keyboard with his finger and breathed through his flared nostrils. "Why are they worried *now*?" He turned towards her.

She hunched her shoulders again. "I told them about your friend."

He shot her a dirty look but kept quiet.

She put her hands up in protest. "But it was in your own defense. They were starting in again about how depressed and detached you had become and..."

Hunter growled. "Dammit! Don't you people understand that I need my privacy? The family was totally against me and Corina getting married and then tried to act so fucking destroyed when she was killed in Iraq. Now, they are suddenly *concerned*? I thought that I made it perfectly clear that I didn't want to be the recipient of their *concern* anymore."

Hanna loosened her balled-up fists and took a deep breath. "Maybe if you would just talk to them, they would stop probing me." Hanna thought it really wasn't her fault but his. He was the one avoiding his family. He was the one seeing a black woman. He was the one who was still sulking so many years after Corina's death. Yet, she was the one who was being blamed for everything.

"And maybe I don't care if they are concerned or not!" He stood up and snatched off his smock. "I'm out of here. Tell the wolves that they can circle if they like, but I'm not defenseless this time. If they try to ruin this for me, I'll cut all ties. I swear it, Hanna." He stared down at his sister and grabbed his keys. "And you had no right to run your mouth about me and Stacey. It's none of your damned business. I don't' bother you about Jack."

"I mourned for her too, Hunter. She was my friend too!" Hanna exclaimed, stomping her foot like a child.

Hunter let go of the knob and put his head on the door. "I know that, Hanna. And you'll probably meet and befriend Stacey, so that you can say that you have one black friend, right? But it won't stop you from stabbing her in the back, looking down on her and making our relationship a living hell." He spoke of possible future misdeeds from bad past experiences.

"I would never do that," she said with sincere conviction. Her pleading eyes locked on to the back of her brother's head. "You know me better than that, Hunter."

He turned to her, but her beautiful face was too wrought with pain for him to stare back into. He looked down at the floor and smirked. "Haven't you already laid the foundation? It was my job to tell Mom and Dad about Stacey, not yours. You're already meddling."

"I was taking up for you," she answered, stepping towards him.

Hunter stepped back. His voice was serious. "I don't need anyone to *take up* for me." Opening the door, he left quietly.

***

Stacey was ahead of schedule by a month. Every time that Hunter left and went to work, she sat in front of her computer and typed until he came home. For hours, she would immerse herself in the world that she had created of the same love and passion that she was experiencing right in her very home. Never before had she been so happy to write and so filled with ideas. Her imagination ran wild; many of the pages were a reflection of the nights that she spent in her lover's arms.

Hearing Rapture purr behind her, she finally saved and closed her document and went to the kitchen to make him something to eat. As she placed the bowl on the granite floor, she rubbed his fur. It was amazing, but just a blink of an eye ago, this little creature was the only thing in the world that she had to show or that would show her any measure of affection. Now, she was bombarded with love.

Standing up, she grabbed the crystal vase on the countertop and refilled it with water. The two-dozen, long-stemmed Vera Wang roses fragrantly filled her nostrils. She didn't even know Vera Wang made flowers, but she did and they were beautiful.

Hunter brought home roses every night. It was a ritual with him. Roses. Take out. And then hours of talking and watching television together or reading her story and skimming the Internet. Then finally, they would make love. They weren't busy bodies, consumed with the outside world. Instead, they were comfortable at home, behind closed doors, alone in each other's company.

She paused in the middle of her thought. Home? Really? Had her condo become his home? He woke up there. He went to bed there. He ate there. He bathed there. He took his calls there.

Still in her pajamas, she walked to the bedroom and opened up the door that led to her massive but nearly empty closet. Half of it had his stuff thrown all over it. Shoes. Clothes. Belts. Bags. The other half was her things, neatly put away. Walking to her bathroom, she looked at the counter to find his razors and shaving cream, his colognes and deodorants and a million other hygiene products lined up by hers. The bedroom was the same. A lap top on each nightstand. Shoes on each side of the bed.

"Wow," she said aloud. "He *has* moved in." Until that moment, she had never noticed. Until right then, he had been a guest, but at that moment, she realized what had happened.

A strain formed in her throat. What happened to *slowish*? Now, they were living together? It had only been a little over a month and yet they were moving at warp speed. What happened to this secure blanket she had wrapped around herself in the form of an agreement? What happened to two-months of a pseudo-relationship and then back to a life where she couldn't get hurt or hurt anyone else?

The front door slammed shut and snatched her out of her frenzy. Hunter walked in, roses in-hand and a smile on his handsome face. His bright smile disappeared as he glimpsed her.

"What's wrong?" he asked, setting the flowers on top of the dresser beside Drew's photo.

Stacey didn't realize that her face showed her concern. She scratched her brow with her thumb and looked around the room with her hand on her hip. "I...I just realized that we're living together."

Hunter walked towards her. "Not technically." He pulled off his sweater and threw it on the bed. "I still have a place, remember?" Though he knew that he never went there except to get more clothes, pick up his mail and check on things. His condo had become a glorified storage unit.

Instantly, she picked up his sweater and walked into the closet to hang it up. She seemed to never stop cleaning up after the man.

Hunter stood confused, picking up on her growing frustration. He spun around to her as she came out of the closet and grabbed her by her waist. "Hey, wait a minute. Come here."

She looked up at him and frowned. "We said that we wouldn't do this, Hunter."

"Do you not want me?" he asked. His grip loosened on her small hips.

Looking into his eyes, she melted. The frown lines above her forehead disappeared, and in the sincerest voice she could muster, she shook her head. "Of course I want you, Hunter. I love you. I'm just..."

He put his cold fingers over her pouty lips. "I'm not going anywhere," he assured. Pulling her into his warm embrace, he felt the fast thud of her beating heart. She was scared. Whispering into her ear, he rubbed her back. "I've been thinking about something all day, and this just confirms it."

"Confirms what?" she asked, wrapping her arms around him.

"I want you to see my place."

Stacey stepped back and pulled at her t-shirt. "But it's across town. We'd have to drive. It's raining cats and dogs outside. And I don't...I can't..."

Hunter stopped her protests. "Calm down, baby." Taking her hand, he led her to the bed. They sat beside each other on the edge. He held her hands in his own and gave a sympathetic smile. "I can completely understand your fear, Stacey, but one day..."

"I knew that this was going to happen," she interrupted.

He held on to her. "One day, you're going to have to face your fears."

"You're one to talk. You've never even gone to Corina's grave site," she snapped back.

"Me too. I'm going to have to face mine. But I want us to be together and maybe together, it all will be easier to face." He stroked her face lovingly.

Tears formed in the corners of her eyes. "Hunter, you promised."

"I promised to be here, and I am. But I also need you to trust me, Stacey."

"I don't know if I can do it. What happens if I freak out and have a fit."

"I'm a doctor. I can help you."

She looked up at the ceiling and tried to bat the tears from her eyes. "Why now? Things are going so great."

"Are they? You were just having a breakdown about my stuff being here. Maybe it would do you some good to hang out at my place for a change. It's a change of scenery...a change of pace."

"You're getting tired of being here, aren't you?" she asked, suddenly forgetting that she had nearly just kicked him out for being at her place too much.

Hunter laughed. Grabbing her, he gave her a big hug. "You can't win this, Stacey. I want to be where you are, but I also want to be with you out in public. Piper and John agreed to dinner this week. They want to meet about fifteen minutes from here. You can't expect to walk. I want you to see my home. You have to move past your fears."

"For you?" she asked, swallowing. Why was she the one having to do all the sacrificing.

He hunched his wide shoulders. "For us." Wiping the tears from her face, he stood up. "But before that, I brought home your favorite."

"Chinese?" she asked, hoping that she could think of way to get out of this by the time that dinner was over.

"You bet," he answered.

***

As they lay in bed together tangled in each other's arms, the pouring rain raged outside. Tucking her face into Hunter's neck, Stacey finally spoke after a long silence. Her groggy voice vibrated against his skin. "I don't know if I can do this Hunter," she said, running her hand over his bare chest.

Hunter ran his hands through her dreads and kissed the top of her forehead. "Of course you can," he assured. "I have faith in you."

"Do we have to do it tonight? I mean, can't we wait until tomorrow?" she pleaded.

"No," he said in a matter-of-fact tone. He pulled her naked body up closer to him. As he moved her, her silky skin ignited new heat in his belly.

She looked up into his eyes innocently and pursed her lips together. "I haven't been in a vehicle in years," she said, as though he didn't know.

"It's a short drive. You'll be there before you know it," he said, lifting her chin with his finger. "Are you still in love with me?" he asked curiously.

"More now than ever," she said sighing. Truth was in her words.

He raked his hand over her shoulders. "I know it's only been a New York-minute, but I feel like there is no one else in the world for me except for you. Because of that, I have to take care of you, make sure that you not only get everything that you want but also what you need."

Stacey shook her head. "See, when you say things like that how am I ever supposed to not give you what you want?"

He smiled exposing the deep dimples in his cheeks. "Speaking of what I want...I want you again," he said, biting his lip. "Just once more before we go to my place." He pushed his body closer to hers and kissed her neck.

Slowly and seductively, Stacey ran her hands down the side of his body to his large thighs and then brushed against his growing manhood. Licking her lips, she grabbed him and stroked his thick erection. When she was sure that he was ready to enter her, she stopped abruptly. "Sex? Not a chance. If we're going to do this, we might as well get it over now, chief," she said, sitting up. "Can't have your cake and eat it too."

Hunter laughed and rolled over in bed. His manhood slapped against his thigh, hard as a rock. "Woman, you're really killing me," he groaned.

***

The rain had not let up at all though a few hours had passed since Hunter and Stacey first discussed the inaugural drive. Standing at the door as she waited for him to bring the car around, she looked up into the night sky and felt a deathly chill that ran down her spine.

"I can't believe that I'm actually doing this," she said in a stark monotone as she held her arms around her.

As Hunter pulled up in his truck, she held her breath. He got out and grabbed an umbrella. The water splashed under his boots as he hiked up the stairs to her and opened the door.

"Are you ready?" he asked with a smile on his face.

"No," Stacey said, holding on to the door. "Maybe this is a bad idea."

"Don't be afraid," he said, grabbing her hand softly. He curled his hand around hers. "I'll be right here with you, and I am a perfect driver."

One step at a time, he led her in the rain to his truck and opened the door for her. Putting her in the car, he locked her seatbelt in and leaned in to kiss her lips. "You know I won't let anything hurt you, right?" He looked into her eyes.

Stacey swallowed hard. She wanted to run back up to the safety of her condo and stay there forever. However, Hunter knew that if he let her go back now, he would never get her to face her fears.

Running to the driver's side, he jumped in and put on a jazz cd.

"You like jazz, right?" he asked, turning up the music. "Are you cold?"

She shook her head and held on to the dashboard. Her fingers trembled. Staring at the wet road, she zoned out. It was a night just like this when she lost Drew. The splash of the water as the cars passed caused her heart to race. Nothing scared her more.

Putting the car in drive, Hunter reached out to hold her hand.

"Keep both hands on the steering wheel," she ordered. Her voice quivered as she looked over at him.

"My hands are on the wheel," he reassured. "Everything is going to be okay."

It was like she had never ridden in a car before. Used to the slow manual movement of her bike, she marveled at how quickly the blocks seemed to move past them. Protected from the elements, they went through the rain with ease in the comfort and warmness of his truck with the music playing to sooth her. Calming her fears, she sat back in her seat and nodded to herself.

Hunter knew that she was talking to herself. He also felt privileged to be the one to experience this with her. Everyone handled trauma differently, and if pushed too much, often the traumatized would shut people out. Stacey, however, had opened up to him, trusted him. He knew that he couldn't ask for much more.

Stacey looked out the window as they moved past her safe area. She looked at the stores and houses that they passed like they had driven to another planet. "Oh, I'd like to go there," she said, looking at a Moroccan restaurant that they passed.

"We'll go," Hunter said with a grin. "We can go wherever you like."

"That would be nice," Stacey said, nearly in a whisper. Her hand found the console. Looking over at him, she wiped the tears from her face, though she tried to smile. "I'm scared as hell," she confessed.

He smiled back. "It's okay. I know that this isn't easy, but you have to admit that it isn't as bad as you thought."

"Yes, it is," she said, sitting back. But she knew that it wasn't. Maybe she was calmed by him being with her or maybe it was that she had made too much of not driving, but she felt somewhat comfortable.

When they pulled into the private drive of the upscale waterfront condo community Hunter lived in, he looked over at her and felt like they had accomplished a major feat.

Stacey looked around impressed. It was definitely a place that she would have picked. The condos were well-built, bricked, and spacey. Each had its own balcony. Plus, it had a beautiful view of the waterway, very much like her own.

After Hunter parked, he walked around and opened the door for her. As she put her feet on the step to get out, he grabbed her and hugged her. Her body was still trembling. Holding her tightly, he kissed her neck. "I'm very proud of you, Stacey," he said with conviction.

"Thanks," she said, taking a deep breath. "It was *different*."

"Nice?"

She bucked her eyes. "I don't know if I would say that it was nice, yet."

He liked the word yet. Taking her hand, he led her to his apartment and opened the door.

"Do you have the entire floor?" she asked, stepping across the threshold.

"Yes. This is all me," he said, closing the door behind them. "Go on. Walk around and make yourself at home."

She looked back at him. The word home made her smile again. Going in his office to check his messages, he left her to formulate her own opinion about his little kingdom.

No one normally called him at home unless it was an emergency, but he checked his phone to find that he had one urgent message. He pushed the button and closed the door behind him.

"Hunter, it's your mother," the voice said. "I haven't seen you in weeks, and I'm worried. Why won't you let me see your face? What is happening? I don't care what it is; I want to hear from you. And Mother's Day is next Sunday. I hope that whatever you've been up to that you'll come and spend the day with your mother. We are still your family, you know. I expect a call soon. I love you."

Hunter growled at the nagging voice that pulled him back to his anchor. Having already spoken to Hanna earlier that afternoon, he knew what was happening. He was being set up by them all. Only he would not allow any of them to mess up what he had in the next room.

Stacey was the only thing in his life that was giving him some balance, and in very important and distinct ways, she had given him closure with Corina. Now the family was back to meddling, the same as they had done with his dead wife. He had to figure out a way to solve this problem before it became one. Hanging up the phone, he went back out to find Stacey.

Hunter had a very warm and inviting home with a Greco-Roman theme throughout. Everything was masterfully designed and reeked of privilege and prestige. The first thing that Stacey noticed outside of his interior was that it was extremely clean, just the way that she liked it. She knew instantly based up on his habits at her house that he had to have a maid, because Hunter was hopelessly messy.

The living room and dining room were under high wooden, vaulted ceilings with large-leaf ceiling fans and receding lights. Below were antique wood tables and furniture that Stacey assumed had Greek or Roman origins because of the columns and intricate iron.

The walls were painted in a muted beige and on each wall were photos of Greece and old painting of beautiful Greek women and men. The floors were shining with mahogany wood and elaborate rugs. In the corners were vases and statues much like her African ones.

His kitchen was very modern with stainless steel appliances, gray and black granite tops and more Greek statues and paintings. The hallways were faux painted in a marble design decorated with Danaides of Argos art.

She stopped and looked at the elaborate console table right before she entered his bedroom. A picture of his wife sat by the lamp. Picking it up, she studied Corina. She was a beautiful woman with classic Greek features. Dark curly hair lined her olive-toned face and larger aquiline nose. Her deep set eyes were wide and bright and her high cheek bones complimented her full lips and pearly white teeth.

Stacey ran her hand over the picture and looked back at Hunter, who watched her quietly. "She was beautiful," she whispered. "I can see why you miss her."

Hunter walked up and took the picture. Setting it down, he took her hand. "You're beautiful. I can see why I love you."

Leading her into the bedroom, Stacey saw which room was the selling point of the upscale condo. The lofty room was painted in a slate marble design. A king-sized bed with a beautiful slate blue and chocolate brown comforter reflected his discriminating taste. The large bay windows were covered in expensive royal empire tailored curtains. And in the corners were stone-carved lamps and large marble lions.

"Do you like it?" Hunter asked as he slipped his arms around her.

"I love it. It's you," she said, wanting to crawl into his bed.

"Maybe it could be *us*," he said, unbuckling the belt on her jeans. He intended to finish what she started back at her place.

Stacey turned to him and wrapped her arms around his neck. Her lips lingered at his before she ducked in for another of his sweet kisses. "We have way too much sex," she said giggling.

He kissed her again, sucking at her bottom lip. "I am a doctor, and I can assure you that there is no such thing as too much sex for healthy adjusted couples," he said, pulling her to the bed.

"Speaking of which, I need to take my birth control. I forgot it earlier."

"Do you take it at the same time every day?" he asked, still holding her tight.

"It's hard enough just to remember to take it at all," she said, going to her purse. She pulled out her packet and slipped a pill in her mouth. "Do you have some water?"

"Sure," Hunter said, standing up. He ran to the kitchen to grab a bottle of water and paused. Walking back into the bedroom, he passed her the water and opened his planner on his desk. "I've noticed that your breasts are just a tad bit fuller, and you've had the very slightest change in mood. When was the last day of your cycle?"

Stacey swallowed the pill and pulled out her cell phone to look at her calendar. "It was thirty-five days ago, but if you read my file, *and I know that you did*, you'll see that I have irregular cycles. I'm sure it's coming."

Hunter bit his lip. They had not used a condom since they started their relationship. In fact, even the first time that he was with her, he had not pulled out. He knew that it was stupid then, but he still did it. It was because of his own actions that he was suddenly suspicious of her small changes. Plus, her pattern of taking her pills would only create more of a chance. He had done everything to get her pregnant whether it was consciously or subconsciously. Maybe he had now succeeded.

Walking over to her, he raised her shirt and looked at her breasts again. He wasn't crazy; they were larger, but that was not what tipped him off. It was more of a gut feeling, an *uh oh, look what you did* feeling in himself. Sitting back down on the bed, he chuckled a little. She could kill him for what he was about to say, or she could be ecstatic. There was a fifty/fifty chance either way.

"Stacey," he said in the sweetest voice he could muster. "Baby..."

"Yeah?" she said, taking off her shirt completely.

"Don't freak out, but I think that we're pregnant."

Chapter Nine

It took him nearly half an hour to get back from the pharmacy in the rain. Soaked, he came running in the condo with a small plastic bag clutched in his hand and a wide grin. The look on his face was sheer excitement. Going into the bathroom with her, he unsheathed the box from its plastic wrapping and perched up on the countertop beside her.

Stacey, who had not said one word since he had broken the news to her, quickly took it and pulled her pants down. Sitting on the toilet, she looked over at him.

"This really would be more accurate first thing in the morning," he explained.

"I can't wait that long, and I can't do this with you watching," she snapped.

Hunter gaffed. "I'm a..."

"Doctor! I know, you've said that like a hundred friggin times," she said as the urine began to trickle down. She stuck the stick in the urine stream.

Hunter stood up and walked over to her. "Don't be scared."

"*Don't be scared?*" she asked mortified. "I could be *pppregnant.*" The words seemed too surreal for her to digest. "Just this afternoon, I found out that we were living together, and tonight, I find out that I could possibly be pregnant, and you tell me not to be scared?"

Hunter took the white stick from her and slipped the cover over it. Sitting it on the sink, he pulled his pants up, crouched down and watched it. It only took seconds to confirm his suspicions.

Pregnant. His green eyes lit up as he looked over at her.

Stacey leaned over and looked at the test. Her eyes bucked and her pouty mouth flew open. "Oh my God!" she said, jumping up off the toilet. Urine splashed against the toilet seat. Turning with her butt exposed, she waded toilet paper in her hand and wiped herself and toilet off quickly then flushed.

"Baby, calm..." he grabbed her. "Calm down."

Stacey couldn't decide if she wanted to cry or laugh. Completely confused, she cried with a smile on her face. Hunter hugged her tight and soothed her. "There, there," he said, kissing her forehead. "It's okay."

"We're pregnant," she said, shaking her head. "What does that mean?" Her pants had fallen back down to her ankles.

"It means that we're going to have a baby," he said, pulling her face up from his chest. Kissing her again, he nuzzled his nose in her hair.

Stacey reached for the counter but felt herself nearly tip over. Holding her up, Hunter pulled her pants up and snapped them close. Walking her out to the bedroom, he sat her down on the bed and stood in between her legs. His eyes were beaming with pride, but she looked completely taken aback.

"What have we done?" she asked, trying to keep from hyperventilating.

"It looks like we just stopped moving *slowish*," he said, lying beside her on the bed. Putting his head back on the pillow, he looked up at the ceiling fan and took a deep breath. "Wow."

"You can say that again," Stacey said, putting her hands over her face.

"I hope that it's a boy," Hunter said absently. "But I'll take a girl."

Stacey looked over at him and laughed. He laughed too. This was incredible. A wave of emotion swept through both of them.

"You realize that we have a lot to talk about, right," she said, moving past her initial response. Touching her stomach, she looked down in amazement. *There was a real baby inside of her.*

"Can we talk after we finish what we started?" he asked, running his hand over her jeans.

"And you still want to have sex?" she asked, frowning at him.

"Why wouldn't I? It's safer than it's ever been now."

Stacey chuckled. "You're impossible. You've got me out in the rain driving around the city pregnant and you want to have sex?"

Hunter pulled off his shirt and hovered over her. "Basically."

***

The rain had finally stopped by the time that Hunter and Stacey had finished making love for the second time that night. This time had been more passionate than ever before. Hunter had kissed every inch of her body, including her precious belly. Holding her now in his embrace, they lay in bed talking about what would be for their future.

"We don't have to rush into marriage or anything," Stacey said, looking up at him.

"Right," Hunter said, biting his lip. That was his next suggestion. "But we don't have to *not* get married, just because we fell in love so quickly." He looked down at her and raised his brow. "It's a thought."

Stacey didn't know exactly what he meant by that. She had learned that many of the things that Hunter said were cryptic in nature. "What about our families? Does your family even know about me?"

"Sort of," he said, clenching his jaw. "What about your dad?" He had to change the subject. His mother's voice was creeping into his head at just the mention of family.

"When he's sober, we talk about you. He seemed to be indifferent about your race. He just wanted to make sure that I was happy."

Hunter knew that Stacey's father was an old jazz man who had spent his life supporting her through his work in the bars. After her mother had passed, he had fallen into deep depression and had gotten drunk every day for over twenty years. He lived by himself now in Harlem off his meager savings and the money that she sent back to him every month.

But he never took nearly as much as Stacey would have liked for him to. Whenever, she sent more than he needed, he always sent it back.

"What do you mean by your family sort of knows about me?" Stacey backtracked.

"My sister told them about you at dinner last Sunday."

"Why didn't *you* tell them?" She sat up and put her head on his chest. Was he ashamed of them? If so, that dog wouldn't hunt.

Hunter debated whether or not to tell the future mother of his child and the love of his life that his family was prejudice. However, he knew that the conversation was coming whether he liked it or not.

"I haven't told them, because I'm angry with them. Things haven't been the same since Corina died." He sighed. "She wasn't good enough for my mom and dad, because she wasn't from a *particular* type of family."

"But she was Greek." Stacey didn't understand.

"Yeah, she was Greek, but she wasn't wealthy enough. In fact, she wasn't wealthy at all. She did it all on student loans and partial scholarships."

"But she was a doctor?"

"Yeah, but she wasn't from the right side of the tracks. They didn't really approve of her until after she graduated from med school, and in truth they didn't hold her in high regard until she was a fallen patriot. Then we were the attention of the Greek community and with all of the concern, they had to change their tune."

Stacey knew what that meant. "Your family is not going to ever approve of me."

He sat up instantly. Pulling her close to him, he moved her wiry hair from her face. "I don't need their approval. I don't need it," he said, shaking his head. "This is about us, not them."

Stacey was silent. She wasn't sure if he was saying it for her or for himself. "It doesn't matter that I'm wealthy. I'm black, Hunter. That is not going to change, and even if it could, I wouldn't change it. I'm proud to be who I am, just like you. However, you have to face the fact that it could present a problem with your family."

"If you were the poorest woman in America, it wouldn't matter to me. I love you. My family has no bearing on this relationship."

She searched his face for even the slightest weakness but found none. He was absolutely, positively sincere. "Well, are you going to tell them about the baby?"

"Of course, I am," he said quickly. "I'm not ashamed of us."

"Good," she said, pulling herself to the edge of the bed. "I still want to meet them."

He looked over at her. "You do? Even after I told you that they are *horrible*?"

Stacey laughed. "Every family is horrible. I'm sure that yours is no worse than my own. Yes, I want to meet them. I want them to know that I'm here, and I'm not going anywhere. Plus, I want to meet this mother of yours."

Hunter liked that Stacey had no problem standing her ground. "Okay. How about Mother's Day? My mother has summoned me to dinner. I'd like nothing more than to show up with you."

Stacey wasn't expecting to meet them *that* soon. She was quickly made to eat her own words. Swallowing hard, she stood up naked and nodded his way. "Fine. It's a date. Do we have to drive?"

"Well, if you want to ride bike there, we can always leave tonight, and *maybe* we'll make it there by Sunday. That's if the whole car thing stopped working for you."

Grabbing a pillow, she threw it at him and laughed. "Ha ha, smartass."

Chapter Ten

Every day since her first ride, Hunter had found a reason to take Stacey somewhere to get her out of her house, and while the anxiety had not left yet, it was slowly easing. Tonight, after hours, Hunter had taken her to his office and performed their first prenatal visit.

It was strange to be back in the office again, because this time, knowing the doctor so *intimately*, everything was dramatically different. Stacey paid closer attention to the modern design of the clinic, the many accolades, awards, honors, organizations and degrees on the walls. She also watched his careful care of her, treating her as though she was made of gold.

"Okay, you're good to go," he said, pulling off his gloves. Throwing them in the garbage can, he leaned against the wall and simply glowed. Finally, he was doing this procedure for his own kid. She didn't know how long he had wanted this. He had been different since the moment he had discovered their little secret, as if he had found the cure to his own cancer. Looking at her now, he silently admired the trusting smile that she gave as she got dressed.

"So we have a little less than nine months," she said, slipping on her jeans.

"Yep." He looked at the floor and smiled. "Have you thought of names yet?"

"No, I haven't been able to wrap my mind around things *yet*."

Hunter knew that Stacey had been different. In some ways, she was distant as if always preoccupied in thought, yet in some ways, she had become clingy, not that he minded.

At night, she would curl up to him and sleep wrapped up in his embrace. During the day, she sat in front of her computer and typed away. In the evenings, they made plans and talked about hopes and dreams that would shortly come to fruition with the birth of their first child. But in all, what he truly desired was to know if she wanted any of this.

In many ways, he took the blame. After all, he was the doctor. Yet, he could not deny his own happiness with the thought that she was carrying his child. This woman that he was still learning so much about would be in his life forever, and while he had never seen her bad side, he was sure that it could not outweigh her good side.

"Hunter, where are you?" she asked, interrupting his deep thoughts.

He looked up. "Huh?" Blinking hard, he adjusted.

"Where did you just go?"

He scratched his head. All of that would be impossible to explain at the very moment. Plus, there was little that didn't require a thorough discussion with Stacey. Escorting her out of the room, he tried to move away from his thoughts. "Nothing, sweetie. Would you like to go and get something to eat?"

"Well, we have to go to dinner with your friends tonight. So, I don't think that I should eat before then." She still didn't know how she felt about this dinner date. It had been so long since she had been asked to entertain other people.

"So, you're still good on going?" he asked, sensing her discomfort. "I don't want you to feel as though you *have* to go." But she did, whether she knew it or not.

Stacey had grown to learn one thing about Hunter, if she had learned anything at all. Even though he was often very sweet, he was pushy. And he always ended up getting exactly what he wanted either because she caved in and gave it to him or he found another way. It could be an endearing quality at times, but it could also be irritating.

"I'm going to this dinner for you," she said smugly. In truth, she would have preferred to crawl up in front of the television like they did nearly every night.

Hunter knew *that* tone. She was getting irritable, as to be expected. Plus, she never liked doing anything that required her to dress up, though he didn't know why. She had an amazing body. It should have been plastered on billboards, not hidden under jeans.

Turning off the light behind him, he closed the door to the room. "Well, thank you, either way," he answered.

Stacey cut her eyes at him and slipped on her coat. "This baby is going to make me fat. Will you still love me when I'm as big as a house?"

"You may gain twenty pounds at most. With the proper Mediterranean diet, you'll lose it all by your first six-week checkup." He kissed her forehead. "It'll take some getting used to, but we'll be fine. And women married to Greek men have always been known to be curvaceous."

Stacey caught that. *Married.* He had brought it up on several occasions in general conversation, which meant that he was giving heavy thought to it. Like she had told him before, they needed to make sure that they didn't rush everything. She looked up at him and realized that he didn't even know he had said it. *Freudian slip in deed.*

As they rounded the corner to head out of the office, they ran dead smack into Hanna, who judging from the startled look on her face, had heard everything. She quickly raised her hand. "I forgot my cell phone," she explained in a squeaky voice while looking at Stacey.

Hunter wasn't sure if his sister was lying or not. Shaking his head, he put his hand on Stacey's shoulder in a protective motion. "Hanna, you remember Stacey." From behind Stacey, he gave a brotherly scowl, forbidding Hanna from being unpleasant.

"Yes, how are you?" Hanna said, offering her hand. She smiled but her face didn't show the same delight as her quivering voice.

"Fine," Stacey said, shaking her hand warmly. She looked up at Hunter, who had a stone face.

"Did I hear something about a baby?" Hanna asked Hunter. She slowly moved her gaze from Stacey to her brother.

Hunter tried to control his temper, but the redness of his face gave him away. He clenched his jaw tight and held his breath before he spoke. "Yes, you did," he said on a heaving exhalation.

"You two?" Hanna asked, looking at Stacey.

Stacey nodded. "Yes, we are pregnant."

"If you say a word, Hanna..." Hunter warned.

"I wouldn't dare," Hanna interrupted, shaking her head. *The family would shoot the messenger on this one anyway.*

"We plan to tell the family when we're ready," Hunter said, moving Stacey past her sister, who blocked their path on purpose. "And we're coming over for Mother's Day. So, I'll know if you've opened your extremely large mouth."

Stacey thought Hunter was being harsh and squeezed his hand.

"I wouldn't dream of it," Hanna promised, pivoting on her little feet to face them. "But aren't I allowed to even say congratulations?"

"Yes," Hunter bit out. He wasn't expecting that but appreciated it.

Hanna smiled at Stacey. "Congratulations. I know what a blessing having a baby can be."

Hunter cooled his heels. He had nearly forgotten about Hanna's miscarriage a couple of years ago. It had happened right after Corina's death. He had felt awful for both her and Jack. Walking back up to her, he took her hand. "Sis, this is big," he said, looking into her wide, watery eyes.

"Tell me about it," she said, looking over at Stacey. She didn't recall the black woman being as beautiful as she was, or maybe she had not paid enough attention to her on the first meeting. Regardless, she could see why Hunter was attracted to her.

"She means the world to me. I don't want anything to ruin things for her. She's been through a lot, and it's all happened so quickly. I don't want to run her off." He chuckled nervously. This was his Hanna also. They had been close their entire lives. He had to make sure that he didn't needlessly trample her although he knew her capabilities.

Hanna shook her head. "I understand. It's serious now. She's carrying a Fourakis." Letting go of her hand, she walked over to Stacey and hugged her. "I'm really happy for you...both of you."

"Thank you," Stacey said, reading between the lines. Hunter would obviously have to explain the parts of this that she was missing as soon as they were alone.

"Great, well I'll see you at dinner *with* the family. Everyone will be there. Mom invited the entire family," Hanna said to Stacey. "And I'll see *you* tomorrow," she said to her brother.

"I'll be here," Hunter said, watching her walk away. *Great, now the entire family was coming for Mother's Day.* This was sure to be even more of a disaster than he had first thought. Hunter turned to Stacey and raised his brow. "That was awkward."

"Tell me about it," she said, walking with him out to the car. "What did I miss?"

"I'll tell you on the way home."

***

Stacey was ultra-nervous about tonight's dinner party. With no friends or family in Seattle, going out for a meal with other people was absolutely alien to her. Yet, here she was pulling up to a five-star restaurant with Hunter to meet Dr. Piper and John Ramsey.

She knew nothing about them except that they were both doctors, married and had gone to college with Hunter. What did she have in common with any of them? She hoped that they weren't snobs. She couldn't stomach elitists. Sure that the night would drag on beyond her ability to stomach it, she surmised that it would be better to just grin and bear it. Holding on to her shawl as Hunter opened the door for her, she looked up at him like a deer in headlights.

He moved into her. "You look amazing," he mused, offering his hand.

"Thank you," she said, stepping out.

To Stacey, Hunter was the one who looked amazing. He wore a black suit and white dress shirt that was cut to show the absolute perfection of his tall, muscular body. His curly hair looked like liquid silk that curled into tempting curls around his face and brought more attention to his dreamy eyes. And he had an undeniable glow, like he was the one who was pregnant.

The valet pulled off in the car, and they headed inside. At the front, by the hostess, stood a tall black man with a low haircut and a white woman with red, flaming hair and lips to match. Both were dressed in conservative black and holding on to each other.

Hunter greeted both with a hug then stepped aside. "This is my Stacey," he said proudly, kissing the crown of her head. "Stacey, this is John and Piper Ramsey."

"Nice to meet you," she said, shaking both of their hands.

The hostess escorted both couples to a table in the middle of the fine restaurant and seated them under a large crystal chandelier. It was packed with Seattle's finest, all in suits and dresses that spoke to their prestige.

Curiously, Stacey looked over at Hunter and realized that he didn't look a bit out of place. This was his type of environment, and he moved well in it.

Shortly after getting settled, the men ordered a bottle of wine and took off their coats. Stacey sat quietly guarding herself. This was her second official outing in over two and half years, and she felt like it was the second of her lifetime.

"Would you like for me to take your shawl?" Hunter asked, wrapping his arm around her seat. His thumb moved against her back.

"Oh, I'm fine. I'm actually a bit chilly," she answered, pulling the shawl tighter.

"It's freaking cold in here," Piper bit out. "They should turn up the heat or turn down the air conditioner."

John raised his brow but kept his eye on his menu.

"So, Hunter tells us that you two are soon-to-be parents," Piper said, offering her glass to the waiter as he approached with the bottle of wine.

The water that Stacey was swallowing at the moment immediately shot up out of her mouth and onto the table. She clumsily put her glass down. Grabbing the napkin, she dapped her face and looked around. "I'm so sorry," she apologized, swallowing hard. She sent a quick and admonishing look at Hunter.

Hunter looked down and smiled. "Yes, Piper. As I told *John* today, we just found out. And we're very happy about it. This is the first for both of us."

"How exciting," Piper said, taking a sip of her wine. "Stacey, I'm a big fan of yours. I read *Love Knocks* from cover to cover. It was absolutely delicious."

John put down his menu. "Can we order before you begin, dear?" he asked his wife.

Piper rolled her eyes, but didn't look his way. "John has read it, too. But he won't ever admit to reading anything but journals and studies. He's boring that way."

"Really," Stacey said, humbled by her compliment. "Well, I thank you for your support of my work. I'm flattered."

"Are you kidding? You're brilliant. But I've bet you've heard that a million times," Piper said, pushing her menu to the side. Turning to her husband, she huffed. "Honey, can you order for me? You know what I like, and I can't read a bit of French. I always say the words all wrong. I mean, honestly, this is the United States. Why can't they write the words out in English?"

"Because then it would lose some of its authenticity," John answered in an irritated tone.

Piper moved on, turning back to Stacey. "I just think the way that you met is priceless. Both of you were in the same place, grieving over loved ones and then he walks up and propositions you. I haven't been propositioned in years. That had to be so romantic."

Stacey wasn't sure how she felt about them knowing the *specifics* of their relationship.

However, Piper continued. "And now you're finally riding in a car again. I just think that's beautiful too."

"It's good not to be an emotional cripple any-more," Stacey said sarcastically. She shot another look at Hunter. *Was he a big mouth?* Feeling the heat rise under her dress from sheer anger, she turned to Hunter. "What I would like is for him to visit Corina's gravesite. It only seems fair now that I've been forced to get in a car."

Hunter paused.

"Oh, I agree," Piper said, ignoring John's now visible pleas to rein her back in to her place. "I have told Hunter a hundred times that closure will never happen if he doesn't go and see her final resting place."

Hunter cleared his throat. "Well, we don't have to get into that this evening." He moved his arm from its protective stance around Stacey.

"Well, we can talk about the baby, how we met, and how I'm basically a literary hermit. I don't see why we can't talk about some of your short com-ings," Stacey slammed back.

"Yes, you'll find that Hunter is a bit of an offen-sive player, but he sucks defensively. He always retreats," Piper said, looking over at Hunter.

"That's enough, Piper," John admonished. His deep voice was stern.

"Is it?" Piper asked, looking at Stacey. "You're an intelligent woman of great prestige and wealthy, I imagine. What is your thought on our old friend?"

Stacey looked over at him and felt her heart warm. It was evident that he was completely embarrassed, and although he deserved to be beaten down at his own dinner party, she would spare him this once.

"I think besides the fact that we have rushed head first into a relationship and now parenthood that he's a really genuine man with sincere intentions. The rest will have to be ironed out."

Hunter's face instantly warmed. He was expecting a tongue lashing not support.

"By you, of course. No one else can ever do it," Piper said, pouring another glass of wine.

"But of course," Stacey said with a wicked grin.

"Are you finished yet, woman?" John asked, shaking his head. "I can't take you anywhere. Hunter probably won't invite us out for dinner for another year, because of you."

"No, I think she's just what we need," Stacey said, winking at her.

"And I think you are just what *he* needs," Piper said, reaching her hand out and touching Stacey.

"Piper and John have been married for seven years," Hunter explained to Stacey as he put his arm back around her. "With three children." He winked at her as if to say, *this is why they're so crazy.*

Stacey bucked her eyes. "Wow. Three kids, huh?"

"Five, four and three years old," John said proudly.

"So, you can always call us about questions that you might have about child rearing, not only because we are both the city's leading pediatricians, but also the world's greatest parents," Piper said, moving closer to John. Their love for each other was evident.

"Well, I'm the world's greatest dad, but Piper is on valium." John didn't hesitate.

"Valium does wonders for the spirit, dear. I never leave home without it," Piper said without embarrassment.

"Oh good, you're here. Now, that my wife has finally broken the ice, I think we're ready to order," John said to the waiter, rubbing Piper's back.

Stacey had to digress. She had expected snobs and had found that Hunter had real people for friends. Without asking, she knew that he had picked this particular couple for several reasons. One being that they were interracial. The second being because of their extensive parental experience.   And the third because the Ramsey's were as weird as they were. Still, she appreciated it.

Hunter looked over at her smiled as he ordered for the two of them as well. His demeanor was a kind and caring as ever. She was seeing him differently now. Obviously, he was more fallible than he was a couple of weeks ago, but he was also more real.   And suddenly for the first time since she found out about their baby, she truly felt safe, like he would be there with her for the long haul as he had often promised.

Chapter Eleven

With crocodile tears in her eyes and a Kleenex in her hand, Valerie read the latest book of prize-winning, bestselling author Stacey Lane Bryant and realized why she was one of the best at what she did. In the last four hours, she had laughed, cried, screamed aloud and nearly fainted from the clever new romantic comedy from one of the saddest women that she knew.

"It's absolutely masterful," Valerie said, talking to Stacey on the speakerphone as she dug out a chocolate strawberry from her Godiva gift bag.

"I'm so glad that you like," Stacey answered humbly. Picking up Rapture, she sat looking out of her window at the bay and smiled. There was a long comfortable pause before she spoke again, as if she had drifted off into another world. "I'm pregnant, Val." Her voice was flat.

"I'm sorry. The line must be breaking up. I swore that you just said that you were pregnant."

"I *did* just say that."

Valerie chomped down on the strawberry and red juice spurted out of her mouth onto her credenza and white, silk blouse. Cleaning herself up, she talked with her mouth full. "When? How did this happen? Were you artificially inseminated?"

"You remember that guy that I told you about?"

"The doctor who was helping you write the book?"

"Yes. Well, we're in a relationship...a serious relationship. And we're about to have a baby."

"Like in the next couple of months? Oh my goodness. I have to get to Seattle."

"No," Stacey laughed. "I have like a little less than nine months."

"How do you feel about this? I mean, from my opinion of your writing, this man has transformed you. This is ten times better than *Love Knocks*."

"Val, why ask me how do I *feel* about something and then tell me how I should *feel* about something?" Stacey put Rapture down. She hunched her shoulders. "I'm happy. I am so...scared," she said with a frown. The truth blurted out like bad gas. "I'm scared too, Val." She didn't know why she was telling her this, but she needed to confess it to someone.

"It's normal, dear. None of us are promised tomorrow, and no one knows that better than you. So, there is going to be a certain amount of hesitation on your part to open up. But you have to give yourself over to love in order for it to work. There is no holding back, because you wouldn't want him to hold back from you. It has to be an equal distribution of understanding, commitment, forgiveness and most of all trust."

"Wow, I didn't realize that you were so *deep*," Stacey said, feeling somewhat motivated.

"Actually, I just started representing Dr. Gail Zawoka, and she's a relationship therapist. I just finished her book."

"Sounds good," Stacey said nodding.

"It is. I'll send you a signed copy. About the other news. ParaWorld has agreed to six point five million to buy the rights to *Love Knocks*. I think that we should finally move on their offer."

Stacey snapped back to business. She hummed. Six point five sounded like a nice number. "Okay, get the lawyer and do what you do best. I'll fly in for the meeting."

"Wait. You'll what? Stacey, you haven't budged, have not given an interview in Seattle except once, and I had to have the news crew come to you. You haven't done a book tour, a phone interview...anything since Drew died. And don't get me wrong, your unorthodox behavior is part of the formula that made you the author that you have become. However, you're telling me that all of a sudden you don't mind getting on a plane?"

"It's new. I know," Stacey said, realizing that she had overloaded Valerie with way too much information in one day. "But Hunter has made me realize that I have to get back in the swing of things if I want to offer our child a full life. So, yes, if he'll fly with me, then I'll fly to New York." She sighed. "Maybe we can stop and see my dad too. I think it's time that they met."

Valerie was speechless but only for a minute. "You realize that this opens up all sorts of possibilities for your brand."

Stacey cut her off. "Val, I'm pregnant, and after I give birth, I'll be a mother. Don't get too creative with my schedule, because nothing is going to come before this baby," she said, looking down at her stomach. "Am I making myself clear?"

"Crystal," Valerie said, ignoring her. "Expect a call from me in twenty four hours about Para-World. They will be thrilled to know that you're ready to play ball."

"Okay. And one more thing. I'd like to make a sizeable donation to an organization called Soilder's Angels. They help the families of wounded military personnel. I was hoping that you could get in touch with them so that we could make a check presentation of some type."

"I'm very familiar with them," Valerie said impressed. "Wow, you really have changed lady. Never in a million years have I expected to hear such wonderful news."

"Yeah, well he's growing on me," Stacey said proudly.

"Sounds like a great guy."

"He is. Anyway, I have to go. Bye Val," Stacey said, hanging up the phone. Checking her pulse, she realized that her heart rate had shot up dramatically with just a fifteen-minute conversation with her agent.

The sun was setting on the horizon, bright with hues of yellow and gold against the blue waters and the green landscape. Taking in the beauty of God's work, she thought about what Valerie had said. She *did* need to open herself up to love and not be so afraid. Sure, she had torn down wall after wall to love Hunter, but how many more were still standing? She didn't want those walls to be the things that kept either of them from happiness together.

Hearing the door close, she pulled herself away from her thoughts and went to greet Hunter. "Hey," she said, noticing something instantly different about him. "What's going on?"

"We've passed the two-month, three day mourning period. You're officially finished with your novel," he nodded. "And I couldn't stop thinking today about our original arrangement."

Stacey nearly fell over. Feeling for the sofa, she leaned against it. "And what were your thoughts about it."

"Does it still stand?" he asked with a frown.

"Which part?"

"The part of walking away if we...you know...no hard feelings." He could barely say the words.

Stacey refused to cry even though it felt as though her heart had suddenly broken. Nodding, she finally mustered enough strength to answer him. "Yes, it still stands."

Hunter rolled his eyes. "So, what would it take to obliterate our original arrangement forever? I mean, what if I want to make sure that it never..."

He was lost for words. Feeling his pocket, he walked over to her. "I can't lose you," he bit out with a growl. "I can't, and the idea of you meeting my family scares the shit out of me. It's this Sunday you know. It's like..." He counted on his fingers. "It's two days away."

Sighing a deep breath of relief, she grabbed his face and laughed. "Boy, didn't we go over this the first time that we made love? Oh my God. I thought you were breaking up with me!"

Confused, Hunter frowned. "What? No. I'm trying to make sure that *you* don't break up with me." He laughed. "Why would I leave you? You're my girl."

"Hunter, you have to stop worrying about your family. I'm a grown woman. I think I can handle them."

"You've haven't met them yet."

"What's in your pocket?" she asked, looking down.

He rubbed his hand over it again and finally pulled out a piece of paper. "This is my attempt to salvage whatever they may damage." He took her hand and walked her over to the kitchen table.

Sitting down, he showed her the receipt. "It's two first-class tickets to Athens. I booked us a suite at an amazing resort right in the middle of the city, but I also plan to take you out to the countryside. I want to show you the true beauty of Greek culture and why I'm so proud of it, and why you'll be proud of it. Especially since your first interaction with Greeks probably won't be a pleasant one."

"You're so dramatic," she said, taking the paper. "Let me see. When is this?"

"It's in a couple of months. Right after we do the check up for the second trimester. I was hoping we could get away for a while. I haven't taken a vacation since I took off to mourn Corina. This could be good for the both of us. You've been working none stop on the book. You need the rest as much or more than I do." He begged her to say yes.

Stacey smoothed her hand over the paper and smiled. "I've never to been to Greece."

"It's beautiful. It's like no other place on the entire face of the planet."

She raised her brow. He was sure enthusiastic about it. "Okay. I'd love to go to Greece and see what you see." Reaching out, she touched his face. "And relax. Mother's Day won't be a disaster. I won't let it be. Trust me."

Hunter kissed her delicate hand. "You're so sexy right now."

She giggled.

"I'm serious," he said, standing up. Walking over to her side, he scooped her up in his arms.

"What are you doing?" she asked as he trailed a kiss down her neck.

"We're going to have as much sex in the next two days and humanly possible, just in case you *do* decide to break up with me."

Stacey laughed out loud as he carried her to the bedroom.

"Laugh now. Cry later," he taunted as he closed the bedroom door behind him.

***

Hunter always marveled at how completely content they could be without doing anything at all. As they lay in bed together, he played with her hair in his fingers and watched the ceiling fan whirl above him. Stacey picked his brain about birthing techniques and tried to plead her case for naming their child a name that wasn't Greek.

"The first and last names have to be Greek. You can give the middle name," he said with authority in his languid voice.

"Says who?" she asked with her eyes narrowed on him.

He looked down and smiled. "Says daddy," he answered.

She liked the way that the title sounded. Resting her case, she ran her hand over his chest. "On another note, I have news."

He waited with his eyes moving back to the ceiling fan.

She continued. "I talked to Val today, and we've agreed on a number with ParaWorld."

"What's the number?" he asked, proud for her already.

Love Knocks was a huge hit. It was the first book he saw when he went into bookstores, and there was always someone in the checkout line with a copy of the plum-colored paperback. The big hook that kept the readers and media enthralled was Stacey's horrid back story and her refusal to travel or do any interviews. She was a conversation piece for most people – aloof and mysterious.

"Six point five million dollars," she said triumphantly. "I told you that it was a good idea to wait it out."

"Why aren't we celebrating?" he said, sitting up. "You're about to make more on one project than I have made in my entire career, and you're sitting in bed like nothing has happened."

Stacey raised her brow. "I'm happy." Her voice didn't reflect it. "I mean, who wouldn't be? But I've gotten used to the money. To me, it really is just a means to an end. All the money in the world didn't save Drew. It didn't take away the anxiety. It did little to nothing for my sanity. I had to move out of my house for goodness sake, into this place, because it just seemed so big after he was gone."

Hunter knew the feeling. Rubbing her forehead, he digested her words. "Wait, you have a house?" She had never mentioned that before.

"Right outside of Seattle. Drew and I bought it when we first moved here."

"There is still so much we don't know about each other," Hunter lamented.

"I know. It could take a lifetime."

That gave him hope. Pulling her close to him, he kissed her lips. "Is that a proposal?" he asked, hoping that she'd given some thought to his desire to marry before the baby was born.

Stacey didn't seem too put off by the thought. Hunching her slim shoulders, she pursed her lips. "I'm not old school. I think that we should get through this before we dive into marriage. Drew and I dated for three years before we got married. You and Corina dated for two. Don't you think we should at least celebrate our first anniversary together before we seriously consider marriage?"

Hunter didn't know if time mattered when it came to them. Rubbing his stubby beard, he pushed his back against the headboard. "I don't want to rush you, but I could get married tomorrow."

Stacey knew that he would, but there was so much to consider, and she didn't want to ruin tonight getting into a *big fat Greek* argument with him.

However, Hunter wanted answers. "Is it because I'm not good enough for you?" he asked sincerely.

"Hunter...no," she said in a strained voice as she sat up. "Why would you say something like that?" She searched his face.

"Because I'm not an astrophysicist," he said with a smirk. "Because I'm not black. Because I'm not as wealthy as you? Because I'm too spontaneous? Because I'm Greek, and my mother hasn't cut the umbilical cord."

"You said that. I didn't." Stacey had to be honest. Pulling the covers from her legs, she ran her hand through her dreads. "What if I said it was because of all those things?"

His mouth dropped. Talk about being blunt.

She raised both her hand in protest. "Not one of those reasons alone is enough for me to...say no. But all of those things together could make for a very tumultuous relationship where we are constantly pit against each other."

Hunter sank into the bed. "So what do I have to do to change your mind? You are carrying my child. We're going to be in each other's lives regardless for the rest of our lives."

Stacey instantly felt guilty about the *baby* part. "I'm not saying no," she said, putting her hand on his exposed thigh. Looking down, she tried to find the right words. "I'm simply saying that we have to plan...discuss all of those things that you just mentioned and more. We have to be a team, because when I do this - when I marry this time - I want it to be for the rest of my life."

"So do I," he said, throwing the covers off his body. "You talk like I haven't thought about any of this?"

"I never said that you didn't."

"Well then, give me some credit. Tell me what I need to do to get through that damned wall of yours."

"I don't have any walls, Hunter." Inwardly, she knew that she did, but she refused to lose the argument.

"You're holding back. I can see it. *I can feel it*," he grunted.

Stacey wiped her face. "You can't rush..."

"I'm not trying to rush you. I'm trying to love you."

"Yeah, well, have you thought about the fact that I'm a little scared? Why *you* aren't scared is beyond me. But I am. And my feelings count as much as yours."

"I would never *hurt* you," he promised, touching his chest.

"Maybe not intentionally." She looked away from him.

"Not at all," he corrected her. "I don't' get it. You were in a good relationship with Drew. It's not like you're some scorned woman. You may have experienced tragedy in your life, but is it really worth losing what's real right now?"

She didn't answer quickly. "I don't want to rush things just because of this baby. This child was my doing."

Her statement confused him. Wasn't he the one who impregnated her, not the other way around? Standing up, he scratched the nape of his neck and looked around. "Look, I'm going to take a shower and head home. I just need to think for a while."

"Is walking away going to solve anything?" She didn't want him to go, but her pride prevented her from saying so.

"If you won't open up to the possibilities, is staying going to solve anything?"

She didn't answer.

Hunter shook his head. Stacey was obviously not going to give him what he wanted this time. Frustrated, he walked into the bathroom and slammed the door behind him.

Chapter Twelve

The pub, TJ Milligans, was jammed packed at happy hour on Friday night. Sitting at the bar, however, Hunter didn't notice the crowd as he slammed his shots back-to-back. It had been a day since he had seen Stacey – the longest of their relationship- but it felt like a lifetime. And the torture of their separation was killing him.

However, he knew that if he said how he really felt to her, he would destroy everything that he had worked so hard to build with the only woman alive who seemed to bring him peace. So, he had stayed away, tried to clear his head. Called a friend. Did all the things that reasonable people do.

Out of the corner of his eye, he could see the very place that Stacey had sat the night that he had approached her. Who knew fast forwarding a few months later that he'd be the father of her first child? "But not good enough to marry," he re-minded himself aloud as he raised his finger to order another scotch. "Because I'm not a fucking black, rich, astrophysicist," he blurted out.

The people sitting around him looked over curiously, but he ignored them. *Screw them all. What did they know?* He thought to himself. *What did they know about love or lost?*

At that very moment, all he wanted to do was get shit-faced and crawl into a cab and go home alone – only because he would never go to Stacey like this. That would just be one more reason to not marry him. No, he couldn't risk it.

A hand gently patted his back from behind, and then the wooden stool beside him pulled back. Looking over, he saw that John had finally arrived.

"What's up, man?" Hunter asked with a lushy grin.

"What *is* up?" John asked frowning. "I thought that you weren't supposed to do this anymore?"

"Well, that's why I called you. I have a problem," he said, sucking in a breath.

"What cha' drinking?" the bartender asked John as he passed him a menu.

"Water," John said, pointing at Hunter. "I'm the designated driver."

"Oh, good. Well, you can have these back," the bartender said, reaching into his pocket and pulling out Hunter's keys.

"Good looking out," John said, taking them. He turned to his friend. "This is the shit I'm talking about Hunter."

"What? I wasn't going to drive. I was going to take a cab," Hunter said defensively. Really, he was never intending to drive, but he was sure that John didn't believe him. Waving him off, Hunter shook his head. "Never mind. Look, I didn't call you here to argue with you. I could have done that with Stacey. I called you here to talk to you about a very sensitive issue."

"Let me guess. You guys are having the race talk," John said, sipping his water.

Hunter's eyes bucked. "How did you know?" He turned from the bar to John.

"Every interracial couple has the race talk. It's just that some discussions last a lifetime."

"So you guys had it?" Hunter asked again.

"Did we have it? Do you not recall when her father disowned her in front of half of our graduating medical class, or was I there at that cookout by myself?"

Hunter recalled. "I forgot about that. Shit, it's been ages."

"Yeah, well, things got better for us once he died. So, we don't talk about it much now," John said, sucking his teeth.

Until death do his and his family apart? Hunter threw himself down on the bar. "Ugh," he lamented, burping up vomit.

John had known Hunter for many years, and in his time as his friend, he had learned one thing about Greek men. They were high on drama. Putting down his glass, he smacked his lips and shook his head. "Well, you can start by putting your foot down with your family, if you want this woman as badly as you say that you do. If she has to deal with your mother, as much as I like the woman, she's going to throw the towel in on your relationship."

"The bad thing is that they haven't even met yet."

"So why are you freaking out?" John asked.

"Because I know what to expect. So do you. You've met them. And they love you, because they know we aren't going to marry. Remember how they were with Corina? She wasn't good enough, wasn't from a good enough family. Her father was cab driver. Her mother didn't have a high school diploma. The list went on and on." Hunter felt exhausted just thinking about it.

"And you don't think that maybe they've learned from that situation?"

Hunter laughed. "No," he said confidently.

"Well..." John sighed. "It's your relationship. *You* have to control it. Before Piper's dad disowned her, I told her straight up that it was either going to be us or her with them. I wasn't going to spend my entire life feuding with people who thought less of me, because I am a strong black man. So, when he disowned her, we already had a plan. We knew that we were going to stick together no matter what. Now, it wasn't a complete happy ending. The old man never came around, but so many in the family did...like her mom who has been a God-send at times."

"Yeah, Stacey said that we needed to talk. Her exact words were that we needed to plan for our future. But I ran hot so quickly until I didn't let it sink in that she was asking me to do the same thing – to stand with her." His head swam. Rubbing his temples, he looked at his reflection in the bar mirror. "I'm fucking up."

"You and I both know that you two are going to fight. You're a head strong Greek. She's a strong black woman. I mean, together, nothing can defeat you, but apart, you guys could potential destroy each other."

Hunter knew that John was right. "Last night, she told me that she's going to sign a deal to sell her rights to ParaWorld for six point five million dollars. It's amazing. I know, but a part of me felt..."

"Inferior?"

"Yes," Hunter said, hitting the table. "Exactly."

"Welcome to the 21st century, man. Women demand equal pay for equal work."

"Stacey is incredible, but it's hard to figure her out. For instance, she has a home, *probably a mansion*, right outside of Seattle that she doesn't live in anymore. I just found this out *last* night. She has made God only knows how much money with her book. But at the same time, she's the poster-child for reclusive authors, right up there with Hemmingway and Wolfe. Don't get me wrong, her place is nice, but it doesn't reflect her income at all. She lives with computer techs and teachers, not movie stars and athletes. Talk about living below your means. She makes more money without leaving her house than I have made in my career. But she's happy just the way that she is riding her bike, walking around the city and taking care of that damned clingy-ass cat."

"You've got a great catch," John said finally. "But if you don't figure this out, you will have *had* a good catch. And when she finally comes out of this thing, some other guy will marry her and help raise your kid. And it will be all because you weren't man enough to deal with your family."

The thought was sobering. Pushing away from the table, Hunter stood up. "That shit is not happening." One more thought crossed his mind. "Did you know her husband was an astrophysicist?"

"I read about him in *Time Magazine* once."

Hunter shook his head. "And to think that I was happy when the local newspaper did an article on our practice. It's hard to fill his shoes, you know. He was a great husband; he was a genius; he wasn't bad looking."

"You're everything that he was except the genius part" John said, standing up beside Hunter. "And you *can* fill his shoes, if you want to."

"His seat," Hunter corrected, thinking of Drew's car accident. "The way that I see it, this astrophysicist had it figured out. Metaphorically speaking, he knew that Stacey was a head strong woman, hence her driving the car, much like she drove their relationship. He knew that she was a powerhouse and just let her do her thing. That is where he was smarter. He let her drive."

John pulled some money out of his wallet and laid it on the bar, then turned to Hunter and leaned into his ear. "You've had way too much to drink, dude." Stepping back, he hit his shoulder. "Come on. I'll give you a ride."

"No," Hunter said, slipping his balled-up fists in his pocket. "I'm going to walk to Stacey's."

"Like this? I thought that you said that you didn't want to ruin things."

"My mom used to always say that people should not go to bed angry. I left her alone last night. I'm not doing it again tonight. I'm going to her place."

"Well, you want me to drop you there?"

"No. I'll walk. I need to clear my head, maybe *plan* what I'm going to say."

John knew his work was done. "Okay, man. Take it easy. I'm going to get to the kids' recital before Piper has a fit."

"Thanks for stopping by," Hunter said, shaking his hand. "Thanks for the advice."

"No problem. That's what friends are for," John said, bowing out of the bar gracefully.

***

Hunter had never been a nervous man. In the past, he had been the confident one, able to work into a woman's emotions and persuade her to his side. However, with Stacey things were dramatically different. She was a quiet woman, who loved peace and tranquility but also who didn't mind expressing her feelings. Maybe that was why she was such a great author. Whatever the case, they had a different type of relationship. In a very non-confrontational way, she could extract utter guilt from him with only her doe-like eyes and pouty, quivering mouth.

Tonight, he didn't know what to expect. He could walk into her condo to find all of his things in a box waiting for him at the door. She could have surmised that their relationship just wasn't worth it. Or to keep things really simple, she could have changed the locks. There simply was no way to tell.

Getting off the elevator on her floor, he eyed her door at the end of the hall and felt butterflies erupt in his stomach. How would he put all that he was feeling into words without messing things up more?

Pulling out his keys, he unlocked the door slowly and sighed. At least she had not changed the locks. He opened the door and inhaled the familiar scent of jasmine and lilac. Rapture was standing on the door mat looking up at him as he closed the door behind him.

"Are you a dog or a cat?" he asked, kneeling down to rub his back. Rapture wrapped himself around Hunter's hands and purred. "Where's your mommy?" Looking around, he noticed all the lights were off.

Great, she was asleep.

Throwing his keys on the sofa table as he passed, he made his way down the hall to her bedroom. Pushing the door open with his index finger, he found Stacey curled up in the bed listening to jazz. Her silhouette moved in the darkness.

"Hey," Hunter said in a rough, scruffy voice.

Stacey sat up and wiped her face. "Hey," she answered in a nasally whimper.

Hunter wasn't sure if he wanted to turn on the light or not. He had never seen her cry before, and didn't know if he could take the first time being because of something he had done. Feeling through the darkness, he went over to her side of the bed and knelt beside her. The moonlight shun in through her open curtains and cast a glow on her angelic face. He reached out and took her hand.

"I wasn't sure that you'd come back," she said somberly.

"How could I not come back?" Hunter asked surprised. "I told you that I'm going to be here, and I am. But it's not because I feel like I have to be, it's because I want to be. I still stand by the fact that I want to be your husband, and I want you to be my wife, but I'm willing to wait and prove myself to you. And you're right. We do need a plan. We do have so much to discuss. But there is nothing that is going to be said that is going to push me away."

Stacey reached over and turned on the light. She wanted to see his face, to read his eyes and know in her heart that each and every word he was saying was true.

As the lights flickered on, Hunter saw how disheveled he had made her. Her beautiful brown eyes were blood shot red and puffy from crying. A large bushy ponytail of sandy-brown dreads sat crooked atop of her head wrapped in a colorful headband, and she still had on the clothes he had left her in the night before.

As she sat on the side of the bed, he stood up and sat beside her. His face showed his immediate concern. She tried to smile for him, but he quickly took her face in his hands and kissed her lips. "God, I'm so sorry," he said, moving his lips from her lips to her eyes. He kissed both of them.

"I have a confession to make," Stacey said, looking into his eyes. "It can't wait any longer."

Hunter paused in fear. What had she done? What had he missed? If she said that she had gotten an abortion, he'd have a heart attack. His hands clammed up, and he was forced to remove them from her face, but he did not speak. Instead, he waited for tortured minutes until she spoke.

She sniffled. "This pregnancy, while maybe not consciously, was my doing, Hunter. The day that we made love for the first time I should have been more careful, but a part of me didn't want to be. I guess that I wanted this in some weird, very unstable way." She retracted. "Not to trap you, but to have a baby or have someone who would be in my life for the rest of my life." Stacey looked away embarrassed. "I took advantage of you, but I promise I didn't plan to do it. This baby means the world to me, but I don't want to start out a relationship with you being dishonest. And if it sounds like it's too much to comprehend or..."

Hunter was elated. She had not had an abortion. Putting his cold hands on her warm fleshy lips, he silenced her. "Me too," he said, nodding. "I could have stopped. I could have used a condom. I could have done a hundred things differently, especially as a doctor, but I didn't. And it's for the same exact reasons."

Stacey exhaled a deep sigh. "You don't know how long I've wanted to say that."

"You don't think I feel responsible for this little person?" he said, rubbing her flat stomach. He chuckled. "The worst thing that I could think of happening to me would be losing you. The best thing that I could think of happening is having this baby with you. You've been nothing but good for me...nothing but good."

Stacey began to cry again, only this time tears of happiness. Nearly leaping into his arms, she wrapped herself around him and hugged him tight. Hunter held her gratefully, savoring the smell of her and feeling her warmness against him. He never wanted to lose this.

"I love you so much," he whispered into her ear.

"I love you," she answered.

"And I'm going to do whatever it takes, you hear me?"

She nodded. "Me, too."

Maybe it was the relief of getting over their first disagreement or knowing that the baby was safe or that they were still together, but Hunter suddenly went from happiness to heat.

Kissing her lips slowly, he first just wanted to be near her, but as his hands rubbed and consoled her, they also began to massage her skin, feel the curves that had landed them in this situation in the first place. Slipping his hands up the front of her shirt, he cupped her perky, warm breasts in his hands, fondling her pebbled nipples in between his fingers. Her mouth opened, releasing a sensual moan that caused him to lean in and kiss her again. She nuzzled his jaw, moving against him. Hunter watched her face, how her expression tightened, twisted in pleasure.

Maybe it was the alcohol that caused his blood to race and the room to spin or maybe it was the heady news that he wasn't alone in his attempt to take his loneliness into his own hands, but he could not sate his growing lust.

Laying her on the bed carefully, he pulled off her pants and slowly pulled down her lace panties to reveal her perfect temple, trembling under his touch. His strong hands rubbed over her first, then found their way in between her slicked hot thighs to her eager pearl. Rubbing his thumb over her aching clit, he opened her wide and slipped a single digit inside of her. Her eyes closed and her head fell back. Holding on to him, she moved against his strong digits and rotated her hips.

Her long slender back arched in response. Clutching the pillow, she panted as she looked down at his tousled hair while he bent to her slicked sex. His breaths on her lips made her moan. Kissing her softness, he sucked in hot skin in his mouth and heard her cry out. Awakening the beast inside of him, he moaned into her quivering body, full of want and need. His lashes lowered, lifted, eyes half-veiled. She tasted as good as she smelled.

As a doctor, there wasn't a place that he didn't know on a woman's body, and as a man, there wasn't a place that he didn't want to explore on her. Taking his time, he pulled off his shirt and nestled below. With her legs thrown over his shoulders, he made slow circular motions with his long, nimble tongue as he held her open with his fingers. He watched her melt into the bed and forget her worries. Her body wiggled under his touch. Erratic breaths caused her chest to rise and fall, pulling his attention from her heated womb to her needy breasts and all the firm skin in between. Sliding his hand back under her shirt, he fondled her in two places at once and witnessed her climax hard against him. Loud screams and shutters proceeded silk that slid over his hands.

He could barely get out of his pants now. Kicking them off beside the bed, he fell in between her legs and lifted her up to invade her throbbing, swollen sex. Feeling her muscles contract, he let out another masculine moan of his own. The tightness of her body around his was pure heaven.

Trailing a kiss from her collar bone to her ear, his hot breath hissed against her skin as he pumped into her body with powerful thrusts. He watched her submit, moving her hips around below him, adding fuel to his fire. Her long dreads now fanned the pillow and her strong nails dug into his tanned back.

His thoughts intermingled with his want. As he watched her body move in sync with his own, he could feel her soul. The power behind her brown eyes moved him more than the flesh below him. At that moment, he knew he was not alone anymore. There were two people who were with him, two people who seemed to care about him unconditionally, and two people who were counting on him.

The thought brought him to tears. Kissing her mouth again, hot salty water burned at his eyes as they fell on to her face. Suddenly, he stopped, hovering over her with a look of clarity. With awe in his heart at how she had totally transformed him, he pulled out of her body.

"What's wrong?" Stacey asked startled. She couldn't follow the raw emotion that had suddenly surged from him to her. "What's wrong?" she asked again.

Hunter got on his knees beside the bed and looked up at her. He shook his head, pushing past the doubt of what she might say. Taking her hand, he stilled his rushing heart.

"Stacey Lane Bryant, would you do me the honor of please being my wife? I don't want to live with you as anything less. I don't want to be with my child temporarily. I don't care about our families, our culture difference or our money. I see the woman that I want to spend the rest of my life with in front of me, and I know that there will never be anyone but you. You may not know me as well as you knew Drew, but I promise to you from this day forth, I will be an open book. I will be what you need, what you want." He took a deep breath. The sweat ran from his neck down to his chest. Looking up at her, he smiled. "Let me fill his shoes. Let me walk beside you. Let me carry you when you are weary and uphold you and your dreams. Let me take away the loneliness and fill your days for the rest of your life with love. Let me be what I am meant to be...your husband."

Stacey was lost for words. Never had anything sounded so sweet. Finally breathing, she exhaled a deep breath. Wiping the tears from her face, she got off the bed and knelt with him. Taking his hand in hers, she put them to her face and kissed them.

"Yes," she said, completely in love. "Yes, I'll be your wife."

Chapter Thirteen

The clouds blanketed the early morning sky with deep hues of gray outside, but Stacey's apartment was filled with sunshine. Greek music played on the radio in the kitchen as Hunter fixed breakfast for his soon-to-be bride while she cleaned the living room and separated the laundry to wash.

Bliss. It was the only word that Hunter could use to describe his world when he woke that morning. It was the only word that he could use to describe the look that Stacey gave when she rolled over and opened her bright brown eyes to him. Bliss.

Stacey dwelled in the same world as Hunter. Humming as she threw a load in the washing machine, she imagined a small wedding on a hill top with a small crowd of close friends and relatives. For the first time since she found out that she was pregnant, she thought about what their child would look like. It was all so surreal. She was actually about to marry again. Whirling around in the wash room with one of Hunter's shirts, she hugged herself tightly and wondered if her mother could see her right then.

"Hey," Hunter said, sticking his head inside of the room. "Breakfast is ready." His smile was endearing.

"On the way," she said, closing the door on the washer and putting down his shirt.

Following him to the dining room, she noticed the drapes had been pulled back to see the morning sky and the waterway in the distance. A single rose had been placed inside of one of her Waterford crystal vases and a quick but customary Greek breakfast had been prepared of black tea sweetened with honey, feta cheese, olives, bread, a bowl of yogurt with honey and fresh fruit.

Stacey knew that he had done all of this for her, because he didn't really eat breakfast, even though it was the most important meal of the day.

Pulling the seat out for her to sit down, he pushed her up to the table and placed a plum-colored napkin in her lap.

"Thank you," she said with a grin.

"You're welcome," he said, taking his seat. With his newspaper beside him, he sat across from her and shook his head. "This is nice, huh? Having breakfast together like an old married couple."

"Well, we aren't exactly spring chickens," she said playfully.

"Speak for yourself." Fixing his plate, he looked over at her. "I want us to go and visit Corina's gravesite today, if that's okay with you." He waited for her approval. *Would this make her happy or put her off?* He wasn't sure.

Stacey sipped her tea and added more honey before she spoke. "Are you ready to do that?" She looked up at him under heavy lashes.

"I am," he said softly.   "I'm ready to move completely on, but I know that you've been on me about it. So, I thought that we could do it togeth-er."

He watched her face, clear of make-up, perfect and unblemished. Her bright eyes flashed with sincerity. "I'm honored. I'd love to." Reaching her hand across the table, she grabbed his and smiled. "I'm proud of you."

"And maybe after that we could go to Tiffany's and pick out a ring...a very special ring that you'll wear for a few decades."

"Really?" Excitement quickly replaced any thoughts that were looming. "Oh, I think *that* sounds wonderful." She had a surprise of her own. "I was also hoping that today we could go and see my old home...possibly our new house."

"Are you ready for that?" he asked with a fur-rowed brow. They had discussed briefly moving in together just a week before, and Stacey had given some resistance. But now that they were engaged, he gathered that she was very open to the idea.

"For us to move in together?" She shook her head, swallowing hard.

"Yes. I didn't want to pressure you..." His voice faded.

"It's no pressure. I think if we got situated before all of this crazy stuff happens - the planning of the wedding, the baby, the marriage - we could see if there is any use for the house, or if we need to sell it."

Hunter knew that either choice would be a colossal step for her. "I think it's a great idea," he said, shocked. "Wow. We have a day planned for ourselves then."

"Yep."

Hunter tasted his food but quickly put down his fork. "You know, we don't have to go tomorrow."

"Hunter, we're going," she said finally. She couldn't believe that he was still worrying about his family. Where they that horrible? At least he had a family. The only person she had in the world was her father, and he was rarely sober.

"Okay," he said, giving in. "We're going." Smiling, he picked up his fork. "We should probably pray over this food." *Especially considering that tomorrow we're walking into the depths of hell*, he thought to himself. His face hid his concern, but his voice did not.

Stacey ignored him all together and bowed her head. They were going to these people's house and setting the record straight. Hunter Fourakis was hers now.

***

The rain was still holding off by the time that they arrived at the graveyard. While streaks of lightning cut through the dark sky and the wind howled about them, for the most part, the day was pleasant. Just right for visiting.

Hunter had called Hanna and gotten directions to Corina's plot, and Stacey had brought flowers to lay in remembrance, but still Hunter felt uneasy.

Sure, he had told Stacey he was ready, but inside he felt his body going to mush. With every step they made through the thick masses of manicured grass, he felt his legs growing weaker and weaker.

Stacey looked over at him and noticed that he had gone completely pale as though at any minute he would either faint or throw up. Stopping, she turned to him and clutched his hand tight.

"We don't have to do this," she assured him.

"No, we have to," he said, looking at the paper. He couldn't bear to look into her eyes at the moment. It took everything in him to get this far. Any sympathy would just weaken him more. "It has to be right over here." His voice quivered. Walking again, he let the wind push the tears that tried to fight their way out. Following the directions, he finally found her simple headstone on a row not from where they had stood. As they walked up to it, he knelt down on one knee.

Corina Maria Fourakis. Beloved Wife, Loving Daughter and American Hero. To Hunter, the words didn't quiet capture all that she was to the world. Putting his hand in his hair, he tried to calm his trembling body. The knowledge of what she had become in the box below made him ligh-theaded. The memory of how she had been burned and mangled made him sick.

He tried to push he thoughts to the back of his mind to get through this. Finally looking up at her final resting place, he ran his hand over the smooth stone. Someone had obviously been taking care of her gravesite. Only, it had not been him as it should have been.

Withered flowers sat in front and a card was placed beside it, wet from being exposed to the elements. It seemed to be such a lonely place, so solemn and depressing. Old people were supposed to fill graveyards, not young beautiful doctors full of promise, denied of children and grandchildren.

"I haven't done such a good job, have I?" he asked aloud.

Stacey wasn't sure if he was talking to her or Corina. Still, she stood beside him with her hand on his shoulder. Leaning down, she placed the flowers in front of the head stone, then stood and rubbed his back.

"Would you like a minute?" she asked.

Hunter looked up at her, saw that she was in tears and felt instantly consoled. As promised, he wasn't doing this alone. This magnificent woman had done so much for him that she didn't have to do. Now this. He was eternally grateful. "I'd like to introduce you first," he said, grabbing her hand. "Corina, this is my...angel," he said of Stacey. He looked back at the headstone. "This is the woman who has helped me to live again, the future mother of my children and my future wife. I just wanted to bring her here to meet what is left of you, because I'm moving on. I probably won't come back. I don't see what use it will be, but I wanted you to meet her once, just the same. I wanted to let you know that I'm finally doing alright."

Stacey didn't know what to say. There was obviously no need for any of her words. Kissing the crown of Hunter's tousled copper-colored hair, she stood up and walked away.

Stacey thought that in a situation as delicate at this everyone needed time alone. A few years ago, she was right where Hunter was, and she knew that seeing the person that he had loved and remembered so full of life buried six-feet in the earth was as final as things got. It was the nadir of mortality.

She had buried Drew on a day much like today, under clouds and rain. She had worn widow's black and cried a thousand tears. She had struggled with the *whys* that everyone had when their existence was suddenly and permanently altered. And finally years later, she had found strength to live again because of Hunter.

Slipping her hands in the pockets of her jacket, she walked towards the car, never turning around. Yes, everyone needed a moment alone on this day.

***

By the time that Hunter and Stacey made it to the rolling hills of the Beckman Heights luxury homes, it was nearing nightfall. Pulling up to her drive, she got out of the car and walked to the tall iron gate that surrounded her old home. Had it really been that big all the time?

Staring at the large, bricked mansion illuminated by flood lights, she marveled at its size. She shook her head in disbelief. The memory could be a tricky thing. Stacey hadn't been here in over two years. She had left this place after a serious break-down that put her in the hospital for nearly a week after Drew's death.

Pulling her key from her pocket, she slipped it into the lock, pushed in the code to her security system and the gated swung open automatically. Hunter pulled up and let her jump inside before they drove up the long, dark drive to the mansion that awaited her.

"It's beautiful," Hunter said, shocked at the size of it as well. He had inwardly half-heartedly expected a mansion, but this place was colossal.

"Thanks," Stacey said in a soft voice.

She knew that it was a dramatic difference from her current home. This was her old life, what she used to be like when she was Drew's wife. In a way, the extravagance of the place embarrassed her. She had become such a simple woman since then, such a far cry from what she used to be before she discovered the true value and meaning of life.

They parked in the circular drive and made their way up the steps to the white double doors. Unlocking the door, she let Hunter go in first as he had previously insisted. After she turned off the alarm, she stood quietly in the foyer looking around her stately home as a wave of nostalgia hit her.

"Care to give me a tour?" Hunter asked, after he had checked a few rooms to make sure that they were safe. He slipped his small handgun back into his jacket pocket and grabbed her hand.

"If I can remember," Stacey said with a grin.

A maid had been paid to come in once a month and check on things and dust. All the furniture and pictures had been covered in white sheets. The marble and wood floors were still shining and bright. Everything was just the way that she had left it.

The living and dining room were painted in eggshell white with white crown molding and expensive wooden maple-colored floors. The halls were painted in an elegant gray with white crown molding and dark marble floors. A grand crystal chandelier hung in the foyer that led up the alabaster spiral staircase to the second floor of the house. All the walls were lined with art from all over the world, speaking to their appreciation for culture.

The sitting room was plum, just like Stacey's condo with a black, baby grand piano and hundreds of old books in the build-in bookcases. The kitchen was a masterpiece with fine granite counter tops and floors, a large oak table, stainless steel appliances and beautiful paintings.

Each and every room spoke to her intelligence, her grace and beauty. Each room told a story of hopes and dreams, of a life that was never allowed to play out.

As they surveyed the old life of Dr. and Mrs. Drew Bryant, Hunter surmised that his future wife and her late husband were a social couple of great taste and prestige. He could see Stacey serving platters of Hors d'Oeuvres to politicians and scientists, authors and reporters alike in designer evening gowns and cocktail dresses that brought out the color of her chestnut-colored eyes and her silky brown skin.   He could see her smile across a crowded room of elite to her loving husband as she talked to wives about her book and where she had purchased her newest pieces of art while Drew discussed the latest finds on Mars. He imagined that he knew the kind of life that she was used to, the life that the good doctor, Drew, had provided.

As they walked up the staircase to the second floor, Stacey led him to the master bedroom. Surprisingly, it was the only room in the entire house that was completely empty.   There was no bed, no lamps, no tables, no pictures.   Instead, it was a large shell of a room with the potential to be absolutely breathtaking.

It occurred to Hunter at that very moment how hard it must had been to make love to him the first time. Without asking, he knew that they had made love in the same bed that Stacey and Drew used to sleep in and make love in themselves. It had been the only thing that she had taken from this place.

He walked over to her as she stood by the window, gazing out at the sprawling back lawn and looking lost. He knew that she was overwhelmed with emotions and memories that she had pushed to the back of her mind for many years.

Pulling her to him, he lifted her chin and kissed her lips while holding the sides of her trembling arms. "It is beautiful," he said, lovingly. "It really is..."

"But..." she said, waiting for the rest of his statement. She knew Hunter Fourakis too well to expect anything less.

"*But* I think we should consider making our own home somewhere else," he said, turning back to look at the room once more. "This isn't us." Even in a whisper, his voice echoed.

Stacey wiped the tears from her eyes. "I think that you're right."

Chapter Fourteen

The Fourakis home was rife with excitement as the women set the tables and caught up on their gossip, while the men gathered outside to finish the customary lamb. Bright sunny skies shined down on the impeccable Olson Sundberg residence on the shores of Lake Washington in Washington Park. With music playing in the background, kids running about outside and cars parked up and down the streets, the festivities were already underway by mid-afternoon for Mother's Day.

Stacey couldn't believe that they lived so close to Hunter's family. She had imagined a long drive up into the mountains or a community like her own outside of the city, but the Fourakis family lived right in the thick of things. They were evidently the last to arrive, or at least Stacey assumed so based upon the cars that had beat them there. As they pulled to the end of the long processional of vehicles, Hunter parked the car and checked the presents for his mother in the back.

"We can still leave," Hunter reminded her with a smile.

"No, I want to do this," Stacey said, opening her door.

Hunter looked down at the large three-carat solitaire on her ring finger that she had picked from Tiffany's the day before and felt pride warm his heart. It looked like it had been made for her finger. He couldn't wait to see his family's faces when they saw his fiancée's engagement ring. It would shut them up for good.

Grabbing the gifts, they walked up the street to the house, where a few people were standing outside on the porch. The men chattered loudly, laughing and joking until they saw the odd couple approaching; then suddenly they all were silent. Their eyes said what their mouths would not. *Hunter had brought a black woman home.*

Stacey held her head up high despite their frowns. Dressed in an elegant pink silk wrap dress with her hair down and diamonds in her ears, she held on tightly to Hunter as he escorted her up the stairs, past his family.

"Hey Hunter, are you going to introduce us or what?" A man asked, who was about his age in a pair of jeans and white linen shirt, opened at the top to show his gold chain.

Hunter smiled and turned around. "This is Stacey Bryant everyone," he said, opening the door. "These are my cousins, Alexio, Christos, Castor and the young guy over there in the corner is Markos."

"Nice to meet you," Alexio, the oldest and most attractive of the cousins said, offering his hand.

"Nice to meet you," Stacey said, shaking his hand gracefully.

"Why are you here with this loser?" Markos asked Stacey playfully.

Everyone laughed. Hunter pulled Stacey inside the doorway and stuck his head back out. "She's my fiancée, you idiot. She'll be around a lot, so be nice."

The men's faces went blank. As they pushed up to the door to get a second look, Hunter closed it tight behind him.

"I thought you had a small family?" Stacey said, quietly observing the droves of people moving around the house.

"My mom and dad have four kids, like I told you. But I have a host of uncles and aunts, and they're all here." Kissing her forehead, he took her hand and led her into the house.

It was a beautiful home with Greek décor throughout, though Stacey expected nothing less. An open-concept floor plan and wall-to floor-windows gave it a modern and eclectic flare, but the old world designs and use of blue and white made it feel like they had walked back into Greece.

The first person to greet them as they entered the house was Mrs. Fourakis. As she quickly passed by the hall, headed to the kitchen, she turned on her heels and came back. In a flowery apron over her St. John lavender-colored suit, she walked down the tiled hallway to them.

"Hunter?!" she said with her eyes on Stacey. Her voice boomed through the narrow corridor. "I'm so glad that you made it. I was starting to get worried."

"How could I miss today, huh?" he asked with his arms opened wide to receive her. Hugging her as she came to him, he kissed her forehead as well. "Ma, I'd like to introduce you to Stacey Lane Bryant," Hunter said proudly.

Mrs. Fourakis eyes were bright with curiosity. Looking Stacey up and down, she finally offered her hand. "*Ti kanis?* Very nice to meet you, Ms. Bryant."

Mrs. Fourakis was a plump woman with a dark olive complexion, big brunette curls with streaks of silver, deep-set brown eyes and fuchsia pink lips. Her rosy cheeks were sprinkled with blush and eyes decorated with lavender shadow. Dripped in diamonds and gold, she smelled of expensive cologne and hair spray. On her feet, she wore a comfortable pair of flats that did nothing to hide her swollen ankles.

"Please, call me Stacey," Stacey said, shaking her hand and looking her up and down as well. Her smile was cordial, but she was already on guard. "And I'm doing fine. I've heard so much about you."

"I hope that it was good," Mrs. Fourakis said jokingly, looking at her son. "You two come in and make yourselves at home. Hunter you're standing around like a guest in your own home. Come. Come." She led them through the house to the dining room table that had been leafed just for the occasion. Several people were already sitting while Rhea and Hanna set the table.

Everyone looked up as Hunter and Stacey walked through the arched doorway. With her hands clasped together and a painted-on smile, Mrs. Fourakis turned to the couple and introduced them. "Everyone this is *Stacey Bryant*," she said, motioning back to Stacey, who stood with her left arm locked to Hunter.

No one knew exactly what to say. They all sat in surprise, glancing back and forth between Hunter and his date. Hunter raised his brow and escorted Stacey to her seat. As she sat down, Mrs. Fourakis' gift bag fell out of her hand and revealed the diamond engagement ring on her finger.

Rhea glanced over and gasped. Looking at her mother, she nodded her head Stacey's way. Mrs. Fourakis walked back over and looked down at Stacey's hand. Putting her hand to her chest, she looked over at Hunter.

"Is that what I think it is?" Mrs. Fourakis asked.

Hunter cleared his throat and sat down beside Stacey. "I was going to tell everyone at once. But yes, Stacey is my fiancée."

"You're getting married?" Mrs. Fourakis looked over at Hanna, who took off her mittens after she sat down the hot potatoes. "Did you know about this?"

"No," Hanna said with a grin. She nodded at Stacey. "But I think it's wonderful. Congratulations, Hunter. You're very lucky."

"Thanks, sis," Hunter said, looking over at his mother, who appeared peaked.

"Maybe at dinner, you can tell us how you too met and how this all came about," Paris said with a snobbish grin. He looked down his nose at Stacey slyly as he reached for his water.

"Maybe...Maybe not...We'll see," Hunter said, drawing Paris' attention. "It will depend on how *you* behave."

Before another word could be uttered by any-one, Hunter's father pushed through the crowd that was gathering at the entrance and walked inside. Wearing khakis and black linen shirt, he snatched off his hat, revealing his shiny bald spot and walked up to his son. Pointing his short, stubby finger up at his son, he growled. "I want to talk to you *now*," he said, ignoring Stacey.

"Fine." Hunter stood back up. "I trust that you won't try to run her off while I'm gone," Hunter said to the collective group. No one answered. That was their exact intention. "Will you be alright?" he asked Stacey. There was no way he was going to leave her if she felt uncomfortable.
Stacey patted him. "Oh, I'll be fine," she said, locking eyes with Paris.

Rubbing Stacey's back, he clenched his jaw and followed his father out of the dining room.

Stacey pointed at the water jug. "Would you mind passing me the water, please?" she asked Rhea, who looked as unpleased as her father and brother.

Pushing the water over to Stacey, Rhea tried to smile. "So, I've heard through the grapevine that you are a writer."

"I am," Stacey said, ready to battle.

"What do you write?" Rhea asked.

"Romance."

"Are you any good at it?" Paris asked, jumping into the conversation.

"They already know that you're a bestselling author," Hanna stepped in. Sitting in Hunter's seat, she took the jug and poured Stacey some water. "Ignore them. They're wolves."

"So, I've heard," Stacey said, sipping her water. "Mrs. Fourakis, you really do have a beautiful home."

Mrs. Fourakis snapped out of her daze and went to have a seat at the end of the table near Stacey. "Thank you, dear," she said flatly.

***

Hunter closed the door behind him and his father, shutting out the men who stood outside to hear. Watching the old man pace back and forth in front of his credenza, Hunter finally sighed. "Papa, what is it?"

"How dare you bring that *woman* into this house and embarrass your blessed mother on her day!" Dr. Fourakis spit out. Sweat started to form on his meaty forehead. He patted it with his hand-kerchief and stuck the cloth in his back pocket.

"Are you serious?" Hunter asked in a raised voice. "*That woman* is my fiancée." He pointed toward the door.

"And this is how you tell the family?"

"I just asked her not even two nights ago. I didn't know I had to call and get permission from you first," Hunter snapped.

"You can't marry a black woman. You are a Fourakis. You have to marry Greek."

"I know who I am, and yes, I will marry her! Dammit, I'm a grown man!" Hunter said growling.

***

The news quickly spread through the house that Hunter had arrived and brought his new fiancée with him. Everyone who had gathered outside in the back near the dock, near the television in the entertainment room and out front on the porch found their way to the dining room to see his mysterious black woman and the ring that rested on her hand. Sitting around like children waiting on a nighttime story, they watched on quietly with pleasant smiles and wide eyes. However, no one was happy.

Hunter's older sister was the first to attack. Chomping at the bit, she waited until she had an audience before she began her sneaky interrogation. "So how did your family take the news about the marriage?" Rhea asked, taking her seat beside Paris.

As if Rhea had not said anything at all, Stacey lazily looked over at Mrs. Fourakis, who was obviously having a breakdown, and felt a tinge of guilt for the woman's grief. "Do you need any help in the kitchen, Mrs. Fourakis?" Stacey offered.

"No...no." Mrs. Fourakis smiled. "We have nearly finished. We just have to add a few minor touches, and we'll be ready to have our Mother's Day dinner." She ran her hand over the linen tablecloth. "Did you get a chance to see your mother for Mother's Day and tell her the good news?" Tears formed at the sides of her eyes. She wiped them quickly.

"No, my mother passed away when I was a young girl," Stacey said, scooting up to the table. "Hunter is lucky to have such a caring woman in his life. You did all of this on your day. How thoughtful." She looked over the large feast.

"You don't have a large family?" Paris asked. "I thought all blacks had large families."

"We *Greek women* love to cook," Mrs. Fourakis interrupted, warming up to Stacey. "Do you like to cook?"

"Not particularly, but I am getting better at it." Stacey cut her eyes at Paris. She would get to him in just a minute.

"Well, if you are going to be married to a Greek man, you have to learn how to cook Greek foods."

"I'm sure." Stacey turned to Paris with a razor sharp tongue. "Paris Fourakis, right? The name sounds familiar. What field of medicine?" She tilted her head and put her index finger on her lip.

"Pain management," he answered.

"One of my lawyers, *who has had me on retainer forever*, uses your practice. Douglas Jackson. Do you know him?" Stacey asked with a smile.

"Everyone knows Douglas. He's one of the best legal minds in the city," Paris answered.

"And a *black* man," Stacey said, winking. "I'm sure the next time that I speak with him, I'll make sure to tell him that I met you. Did you know that he's the president of the NAACP in the greater Seattle area? His entire family is practically card-carrying, lifetime members. His father is one of the best civil rights lawyers on the west coast. He moved up here from LA."

Paris understood the threat. Douglas had referred countless people to his practice over the years. To have the man come out publicly against him would ruin his business.

Stacey knew that she had made her point. "Why don't you ask *him* on his next visit if he has a large family and tell him about your little theory. I'm sure he'll be quite interested to hear what you have to say?" Seeing that Paris had been muzzled, Stacey turned back to Mrs. Fourakis. "I was married before. He passed away around the same time that Corina did. He died in the rain in a car accident headed to a book signing."

"I am so sorry to hear that. What did he do for a living?" Mrs. Fourakis asked, patting Stacey's hand.

"He was one of the country's leading astrophysicists. He was a member of the launch team that

sent the first aircraft to Mars a few years back."
Stacey sighed and looked up at the chandelier
above her. "He was a good man."

The room buzzed with intrigue. Mars? *Who
was this woman?* Suddenly, *medicine* didn't sound
as important as *space travel*.

Stacey looked around and continued. "And to
answer your question...Rhea. It is *Rhea*, isn't it? I
haven't told my family, which only consists of my
father. He's back in Harlem. I plan to take Hunter
to see him while I'm out there next month."

"Oh, how wonderful," Mrs. Fourakis said,
picking up on Stacey's ability to control the room
with ease. Everyone had suddenly gone docile.

Still in shock, Rhea didn't respond. Instead, she
looked over at her brother who had gone pale.
Evidently this Douglas person had some serious
clout in Paris' life. This was the first time in years
she had seen him speechless.

"Yes, I'm going to sign my rights over to Para-
World for my first book, *Love Knocks*." Stacey
leaned over theatrically. "We finally settled at six
point five million dollars last week. It was such a
relief to get that over with." She turned back to
Paris. "Douglas will be handling some of the legal
components of the deal."

Stacey had one intention, to make them see that
they were all just people and that no one in the
room was any better than she. She knew that it
went completely against her current humble way of
life to boast on such a ridiculous level, but she also

knew that sometimes in order to win, one had to fight fire with fire.

"That's your book?" A woman said from across the room. "I see that book every time that I'm in the bookstore."

Stacey smiled proudly. "That's me, but after Drew's death, I completely shut out the outside world. Now, with Hunter's help, I'm *reintegrating*. No pun intended." She grinned and pushed the water jug to Mrs. Fourakis, who took the jug and poured herself a glass of water. "He's a great man, and he cares an awful lot about you. That is why today was so important for him. He's seeking something that only you can give, Mrs. Fourakis."

"What is that dear," Mrs. Fourakis asked.

Stacey leaned in and whispered to make sure that no one else could hear her. "Your blessing, of course."

Stacey knew that she had made her point, and with Hunter never being the wiser. She had, after all, been the wife of an astrophysicist and entertained the governor, senators and other doctors of prestige at her own home. If there was one thing she could do, it was hold her own.

***

"Think of what you are doing to your family? To mix cultures like this, it's absurd," Dr. Fourakis battled Hunter.

"Cultures my ass. We had the same conversation about Corina and how she wasn't good enough because her father drove a taxi!" Hunter put up his hands. He was done with the miserable man and this miserable conversation. "Don't you see that I don't need your approval? You will need me long before I need you. And since you can't accept her, then you won't be seeing me."

"This is the road you have chosen?" Dr. Fourakis exploded. "To walk away from everything you have been taught to be with some black romance writer?"

"Yes, it is. She is my life now – not you. Now, I'm going to get my fiancée and get the hell out of here. You can explain to Mom why her Mother's Day was ruined and why you just lost a son," Hunter said, grinding his teeth.

"I did what you did once. I started to accept this culture and forget my own. That is how you and your sister ended up with *American* names instead of strong Greek names. It's why you are so full of these *American* ideas about family, marriage and life. But trust me, boy. You will come running back to your Greek heritage long before this world bends to your will. This marriage will never work. It should never happen," Dr. Fourakis said angrily.

Hunter walked to the door and stopped. Turning around, he shook his head. "She's carrying your only grandchild. It's a shame that you'll never see him. You would rather hold on to your *culture* than embrace your family. The only thing I see here is a tragic old man." Opening the door, he pushed past the men who eavesdropped outside and went to the dining room to collect Stacey.

As he entered, Mrs. Fourakis and Stacey were laughing along with the rest of the room. *And to think that he was actually worried about leaving her alone.* Walking up to the table, he kissed his mother on the head and then leaned over to Stacey's ear. "We're leaving now," he said, grabbing her hand gently.

"But we just got here." Stacey looked up confused.

Dr. Fourakis came barreling back through the door and made eye contact with his wife, who looked over at him angrily. Now Hunter was leaving? "What have you said to him?" she asked, standing up.

All eyes turned to Dr. Fourakis. "I told him the truth. This marriage can never be. But now I know why he wants to do it so badly." He looked over at Stacey. "She's pregnant."

Hunter helped Stacey with her purse and ignored his father. Pushing her seat up, he headed with his fiancée out through the back way. He'd get out of this place if it was the last thing that he did.

"Pregnant?" Mrs. Fourakis said with tears in her eyes. Turning to Hunter, she pleaded. "Wait! Wait! Please!"

Hunter stopped and turned around with Stacey locked in his embrace. This was his mother. He could stand to scream at the old man all day, but there was no way he could be too cruel to his loving mother.

Mrs. Fourakis moved from the table over to him quickly. "Don't go," she said, touching his face. "I know what troubles we put you through with Corina, but as your mother I promise, you will not face them this time." She looked over at Stacey. Tears ran down her cheeks. "I have no grandchildren. Not one. If what my husband is saying is remotely true, then you have both given me the best mother's day gift I could ask for." She motioned back at the table. "Please...don't go. You are welcome in my home. You are my son. She's is your future wife. You are welcome here." Her voice cracked with pain. Tugging at her son's arm, she tried to get him to sit as the tears rushed down her face.

Hunter did not move. "And what about him?" he asked, looking at his father.

"My word has not changed," Dr. Fourakis said, still standing at the doorway.

"Then neither will mine," Hunter said, holding Stacey's hand. He pulled it up to him and kissed it. Looking into her eyes, he smiled. "It's just you and me." All eyes focused on the couple. Not a single sound was made, except for Mrs. Fourakis' sniffling.

Stacey shook her head silently. She knew that from the very beginning, but she was hoping to come here and pull one ally. Looking at Mrs. Fourakis, she knew that maybe she had managed to do that. Stacey knew that the woman loved her son and would do anything to keep him in her life.

Hunter turned to his mother and kissed the crown of her head. Smelling her perfume, he hugged her tight. "I love you, Ma," he whispered. "But you and I will have to celebrate some other time. Maybe you can come over and teach Stacey how to fix a good Greek meal."

Mrs. Fourakis cried. Holding on to her son, she shook her head. "I'm so sorry, Hunter. I'm so very sorry."

Hanna watched with tears in her own eyes. She looked around at Paris, Rhea and her father in disgust. *What had they done?*

"It's okay," Hunter said, pulling away. Giving his mother a reassuring, bright smile, he touched her chin. "I'll call you, okay?"

Mrs. Fourakis nodded. "I'll be waiting."

Taking her hand again, Hunter led Stacey out of the house. He had said what he had to say. This was his wife, his life, his choice and no one was going to take that away from him – not even them.

Epilogue

One Year Later...
Santorini, Greece

120 miles from Greece's mainland on a sunny picturesque Saturday evening, the bells of the Orthodox Metropolitan Cathedral boomed through Fira as the doors of the majestic white church opened to present to the world Dr. and Mrs. Hunter Fourakis.

Running out, hand-in-hand in the warm tranquil breeze with close friends and family following with cheers, Hunter and Stacey kissed on the steps of the church and waved at baby Corina before they loaded into their white Mercedes and zipped off down the cobblestone streets of the seaside city to the first-class Aressana Hotel.

Cuddled up in each other's arms in the back of the car, Stacey looked up at her new husband and smiled. Her long elegant gown flowed around her brightening her glowing face and sandy dreads pulled up into beautiful curls on her head.

"We did it," she said, rubbing through his copper-colored curls.

"I know. How does it feel to be Mrs. Fourakis?" he asked, kissing her lips again.

"Wonderful," she said, beaming with joy. "Do you think baby Corina will be okay with your parents for an entire week?"

"Are you kidding? Did you see them? Papa and Mama where practically fighting to hold her. Trust me. She'll be fine...maybe a little more spoiled when we get her back. But for right now, I just want you to relax. It's our honeymoon. We're going to get massages, eat great dinners, watch the sunset, make love and spend some much needed downtime alone."

Stacey loved the way that sounded.

The last year had been an absolute world wind. With the release of her second book, which instantly became a hit and a *USA Today* and *New York Times* bestseller, she had gone on an extensive book tour right before Corina's birth. However, she had warned Valerie, who had even shown up to the wedding, that the tour would be the last for a while.

Stacey had also been on the set of *Love Knocks* as a consultant and preparing for the movie to hit theatres in a month. And because of their trip last year to Athens, Stacey, Hunter and Rapture had permanently relocated to Greece to raise baby Corina.

As it turned out, Hunter had been right. While Stacey had visited France, England, South Africa and Spain before, she had never seen a place more beautiful than Greece. It was biker's paradise and writer's utopia. Every day, she found herself overwhelmed with ideas, never wanting for passion again.   The people were warm and welcoming, always interested in sharing their culture and learning more about hers. She couldn't believe it, but she was actually becoming an extrovert again.

When she agreed to move to Greece, Hunter quickly shut up shop in Seattle and started a small doctor's office in the heart of Athens, not far from their new home, a villa with red rooftops, a sprawling lawn and plenty of space for future Fourakis babies. Their new life was like a dream. God had blessed them with a piece of heaven right here on earth, and they treasured every moment of it.

Corina had given them new energy with her birth. A fat, bubbly child with copper-colored curls and emerald green eyes like her father and an angelic golden bronze complexion, perfect heart-shaped lips and her mother's humor, she was the apple of her parents' eyes.

When they were not working, they spent their days doting after her, taking walks, riding bikes, shopping in the markets and watching her grow. Their evenings were devoted to cooking great Mediterranean meals, reading good books, entertaining their new friends and being a family.

The only thing in life Hunter wanted that he didn't have was marriage to bind him to his perfect family. Stacey had insisted that they wait until after Corina's birth to ensure that they could enjoy their honeymoon. At first, he thought she had just found a way to put him off again, but after he saw her walk down the aisle this afternoon in her angelic white dress, he knew that it was worth the wait.

Stacey had felt the exact same joy as she stood beside him at the altar. Never had Hunter been more handsome than in his black tuxedo. His hair smelled of a fragrance that she couldn't place, his skin smelled of sandalwood. His olive-colored skin was toned, vibrant and absolutely beautiful. His eyes shimmered like the Aegean Sea. And he and baby Corina were all hers for the rest of her life.

As Hunter had often put it, the two had finally found their *Opa*, and nothing could have made them happier.

The End

Trivi's Charities of Choice

There are so many worthy charities that need your help. Please consider making a contribution to the following charities to help military men and women and their families in their time of need.

Semper Fi Fund
http://semperfifund.org/
Wounded Warrior Center · Bldg H49 ·
Camp Pendleton, CA 92055
Phone: 760-207-0887
or 760-725-3680
Fax: 760-725-3685

Soldier's Angels
http://www.soldiersangels.org/
1792 E Washington Blvd
Pasadena, CA 91104

Wounded Warrior Project
http://www.woundedwarriorproject.org/
4899 Belfort Road, Suite 300
Jacksonville FL, 32256
Telephone: 877.832.6997
Fax: 904.296.7347

Whether time or money, consider giving back to the people who have already given so much.

STAY IN TOUCH

Official Author Website
www.latrivianelson.info

Email Latrivia Today
Latrivia@LatriviaNelson.com

Follow Latrivia on Twitter
www.twitter.com/Latrivia

Blog With Other Lonely Heart Fans
www.thelonelyheartseries.wordpress.com

"Like" The Lonely Heart Series
www.facebook.com/thelonelyheartseries

Become Friends on Facebook
www.facebook.com/latrivia.nelson

Visit Latrivia's YouTube Channel
www.youtube.com/Latrivia2009

The Grunt

Staff Sergeant Brett Black has a bad feeling that something is going to go terribly wrong. And as a Recon Marine, he pays attention to

his gut. Only nothing can prepare him for what he encounters when he arrives at home from the base. His wife is leaving him, and there is nothing he can do about it.

Abandoned with a kid, the super alpha-male has to become domesticated quickly or find a willing substitute to help him with his son. Only the substitute he finds is no substitution.

Courtney Lawless is a true wild card. The budding librarian loves the classics and carries herself like a lady by day. But she also is full of life and surfs the waves of the Atlantic Ocean by night. Since her parents won't pay for college because of bad decisions in her past, the reformed bad-girl takes a job as

Brett's live-in nanny to finish paying for school.

Brett has never seen a woman of such complex duality. Used to a wife who won't clean, cook or even talk to him, when he starts to live with Courtney, he realizes what he's been missing his entire life. Educated, amazing and refreshingly honest, the only thing that that this transparent beauty hides from her new boss is that she's also the Lieutenant Colonel's daughter.

Faced with another deployment to Afghanistan soon, the brooding Marine is forced to come out his shell to fight for what he loves, only this time, the war is at home.

Enjoy the interracial must-read romance of the summer, The Grunt, the third a longest book in Latrivia S. Nelson's Lonely Heart Series and today.

Third Book Book In Lonely Heart Series
ISBN: 978-0-9832186-4-7
Retail Price: $8.99

The Ugly Girlfriend

LaToya Jenkins is the quintessential woman: smart, successful, grounded and determined. She only has one problem socially - she's overweight. As the "big

one" of her girlfriends, she often faces rejection from the men of their social circle because of her size and/or her dark skin. And due to a painful past relationship, she gives up on love completely until, she takes on Mitchell "Mitch" O'Keefe as a new client.

The Irish born architect needs a professional cleaning service to help him literally clean up his life after a nasty divorce, but he winds up finding a true friend in LaToya, the owner of It's An Honor Cleaning   Service.

While LaToya is handicapped emotionally by her baggage, Mitch thinks she's the strongest woman he's ever seen and a breath of fresh air in his hectic life. His only goal is to prove to her that his interest in her is more than lust sparked by curiosity.

Read the story of two beautiful people in totally opposite ways who help each other see that beauty is not skin deep but soul deep in the first book of Latrivia S. Nelson's Lonely Heart Series, The Ugly Girlfriend.

The Lonely Heart Series
Book One
ISBN: 978-0-9832186-4-7
Retail Price: $9.99

Dmitry's Closet

From author Latrivia S. Nelson, author of the epic romance Ivy's Twisted Vine, comes a story about Memphis, TN, a deadly faction of the Russian mafia and an innocent woman who dismantles an empire.

Orphaned virgin Royal Stone is looking for employment in one of the country's toughest recessions. What she

finds is the seven-foot, blonde millionaire Dmitry Medlov, who offers her a job as the manager of his new boutique, Dmitry's Closet. After she accepts his job offer, she soon accepts his gifts, his bed and his lifestyle. What she does not know is that her knight in shining armor is also the head of the Medlov Organized Crime Family, a faction of the elite Russian mafia organization, Vory v Zakone.

Falling in love with the clueless Royal makes Dmitry want to break his coveted code, leave his self-made empire and start a life far away from the perils of the Thieves-in-Law. Only, his brother, Ivan, comes to the Memphis from New York City bent on a murderous revenge.

With the FBI and Memphis Police Department working hard to build a case against Dmitry and his brother trying to kill him, he is forced to tell Royal of his true identity, but Royal also is keeping a secret - one that changes everything.

Who will win? Who will lose? Who will die? Watch all the skeletons as they tumble out of the urban literature sensation Dmitry's Closet.

Warning: This book contains graphic language, sex, and various forms of violence. However, it will also melt your heart!

The Medlov Crime Family Series
Book One
Available in paperback and e-book format
ISBN: 978-1-6165874-5-1
Retail Price:$12.99

Dmitry's Royal Flush: Rise of the Queen

From the popular multicultural author, Latrivia S. Nelson, comes the highly anticipated second installment of the Medlov Crime Family Series, Dmitry's Royal Flush: Rise of the Queen.

For Dmitry and Royal Medlov, money doesn't equal happiness. Forced to leave Memphis, TN and flee to Prague after a brutal mafia war, the couple nestled into the countryside to raise their daughter, Anya, and lead a safe, quiet life. But when Dmitry's son, Anatoly, shows up with an offer he can't refuse, Dmitry is forced to go back to the life he left as boss of the most feared criminal organization in world. Consequently, the deal could not only destroy the Medlov Crime Family but also Dmitry and Royal.

Royal hasn't been the same since she was attacked three years ago. Where she used to be a sweet, innocent girl, she's now the jaded, bitter mistress of the Medlov Chateau. However, a reality check is in store for the pre-Madonna when Anya's new teacher shows up with her sights set on stealing Dmitry, and Ivan's old ally shows up with his sights on killing him. Can Royal save them all? Will she?

With a family in such turmoil, the only way to survive is to stick together. Read the gripping tale of a marriage strong enough to stand the test of time as Dmitry realizes that he has the best cards in the house as long as he has a Royal Flush.

The Medlov Crime Family Series
Book Two
Available in paperback and e-book format
ISBN: 978-0-5780601-1-8
Retail Price: $13.99

Anatoly Medlov: Complete Reign

From the bestselling series, the Medlov Crime Family, comes the highly-anticipated story about America's favorite bad boy...

Anatoly Medlov is the youngest crime boss in the Medlov

Organized Crime Family's history. Now, he has to prove himself to a council who thinks his legacy has not been well-earned, amidst a grueling investigation by Lt. Nicola Agosto of the Memphis Police Department and during plot to destroy him by his ex-lover, Victoria. In his loneliness, the only one he can confide in is the shop girl, Renee, an old friend who knows more than anyone about his personal journey. However, his friendship soon turns to love for a woman he knows that he cannot have because of the feared code his is bound to by the Vory v Zakone.

When his estranged mother dies suddenly, Anatoly flies to Russia to pay his last respects and discovers a jolting secret.

The late Ivan Medlov's own brutal legacy still lives through his son, Gabriel, and his New York crime family. Anatoly's father and former Czar of the underworld, Dmitry, sees this as an opportunity to unite the two major families and blesses both men. However, Anatoly sees Gabriel as a threat to his empire and competition for the affection of his father. Will cousins kill because of the sins of their fathers?

Gabriel Medlov has always resented his existence. Now as an undercover DEA agent, he plans destroy the Medlov Crime Family once and for all. Only in order to get close enough to destroy the organization, he must also get close enough to love his estranged family. Will blood prove thicker than water or will one man's revenge end the Family for good?

Follow the story of one young man who fights to be king in a room full of royalty and suffers the pain of his position in the romantic suspense guaranteed to make you want more.

The Medlov Crime Family Series
Book Three
Available in paperback and e-book format
ISBN: 978-0-9832186-1-6
Retail Price: $14.99

Upcoming Books

The Lonely Heart Series:
Gracie's Dirty Little Secret
Taming the Rock Star
Unleashing the Dawg
The Pitcher's Last Curve Ball
The Tragic Bigamist
The Credit Repairman

The Medlov Series:
Saving Anya

The Chronicles of Young Dmitry Medlov:
Volume 4-8

The Agosto Series:
The World In Reverse

The Married But Lonely Series:
Forgive Me
Sexting After Dark

Paranormal Books
Funny Fixations
The Guitarist
The Pain of Dawn

The Nine Lives of Kat Steele:
Volumes 1-9

*Books will be released during 2011 & 2012, but dates are tentative so please visit website for updates.

About the Author

In the last three years, bestselling author Latrivia S. Nelson has published ten novels including the largest interracial romance novel in the genre to date, *Ivy's Twisted Vine* (2010), The Medlov Crime Family Series and The Lonely Heart Series. She is also the President and CEO of RiverHouse Publishing, LLC, the wife of retired United States Marine Adam Nelson, the mother of two beautiful, rambunctious children and working diligently on her Ph.D.

When she's not busy writing novels, doing homework or running a publishing company, Nelson spends her time at princess tea parties with her daughter, Tierra, or being saved by her super hero son, Jordan, during playtime, cooking great meals for the family and watching the sunset with her best friend and real-life super hero, Adam.

Attention Future Romance Authors:

Do you have a romance novel or short story that you want to share with the world? Is it edgy? Is it romantic? Is it erotic? Is it unpublished?

Latrivia S. Nelson and RiverHouse Publishing are going to launch a **e-book only imprint** in the Summer of 2012, Love Only.

We will begin accepting submission in January 2012 and will announce the authors in April of 2012. For more information, please contact Latrivia S. Nelson via email at Lnelson@RiverHousePublishingLLC.com.

The Home of Bold Authors with Bold Statements.

www.riverhousepublishingllc.com

RIVERHOUSE
PUBLISHING

CPSIA information can be obtained at www.ICGtesting.com
Printed in the USA
LVOW112039300512

283859LV00003B/5/P

9 780983 218692